# ☠ ADVENTURES IN ☠
## PIRATE COVE
### THE DESPERATE ESCAPE

MARTYN GODFREY is an ex–junior high teacher who wrote his first book on a dare by one of his students. Since that time, he has written nearly thirty books for young people. Many of the humorous incidents in his stories originate from his fan mail. ''I get lots of letters from young people,'' he explains. ''Most of them tell me of a funny experience. It's great reading about the silly things that happen to people.'' Besides writing, Martyn's hobbies include growing older and collecting comic books.

# ☠ ADVENTURES IN ☠
# PIRATE COVE
## THE DESPERATE ESCAPE

# MARTYN GODFREY

AN AVON  CAMELOT BOOK

VISIT OUR WEBSITE AT
http://AvonBooks.com

ADVENTURES IN PIRATE COVE #3: THE DESPERATE ESCAPE is an original publication of Avon Books. This work has never before appeared in book form.

AVON BOOKS
A division of
The Hearst Corporation
1350 Avenue of the Americas
New York, New York 10019

Copyright © 1997 by Martyn Godfrey
Published by arrangement with the author
Library of Congress Catalog Card Number: 96-96489
ISBN: 0-380-77504-2
RL: 4.9

First Avon Camelot Printing: January 1997

CAMELOT TRADEMARK REG. U.S. PAT. OFF. AND IN OTHER COUNTRIES, MARCA REGISTRADA, HECHO EN U.S.A.

Printed in the U.S.A.

OPM   10   9   8   7   6   5   4   3   2   1

*To Bev Finlay and Mr. Fitz*
*and their wonderful students in Keenooshayo School . . .*
*thanks for all the help.*

## chapter 1

**"** If you don't close your mouth, Garrett, a bird is going to make a nest in there," Stacey teased.

"Sorry," I said. "I was thinking of something."

"Thinking how good-looking Leighla Livingston is?" Stacey asked.

"Not really." Actually, that's exactly what I *was* thinking. My girlfriend, Stacey, and I were watching TV in my living room and a Leighla Livingston commercial was on. Usually, I don't give a hoot about designer jean commercials. But ever since Leighla Livingston has been doing them, I pay attention. Leighla Livingston is the hottest child supermodel. It seems as if she's in every second ad. And she's only my age.

My friend Delton thinks Leighla Livingston is the best-looking eighth grade girl in the whole

1

world. There's no way I can disagree. 'Course, I'd never tell Stacey that.

"What I'd give to look like Leighla Livingston," Stacey said.

"She's not all that great," I said diplomatically.

Stacey looked at me like I'd lost my mind. "How can you say that, Garrett? She's gorgeous. When my cousin Butcher sees her on TV, he drools on his T-shirt."

I laughed. "There's nobody like Butcher."

"She looks like she's smiling and pouting at the same time," Stacey said. "What I'd give to have a smile like that."

"Your smile is a lot like Leighla Livingston's," I pointed out.

Stacey's face dissolved. "What a nice thing to say, Garrett."

I'm Joe Smooth, I thought.

"Hi, guys. What are you watching?" my little brother, Hornbeck, asked as he walked into the room.

"A Leighla Livingston commercial," Stacey answered.

"Oh, yeah, the pretty girl," Hornbeck said. "Are the mystery guests here yet?"

"Not yet."

"Mystery guests?" Stacey asked.

"It's some big secret. We have no idea who they are, but they've rented all three guest rooms in

Bed and Roses. The person who made the reservation said they had to have complete privacy. Definitely strange. They should be here any minute."

"It's got to be somebody really famous," Hornbeck said.

"Where you been, Bro?" I wondered. "With Travis?"

"Naw, I was kissy-facing with my girlfriend."

Stacey scrunched her eyebrows. "Kissy-facing?"

"My grandmother's way of saying hugs and kisses."

Stacey looked more confused. "Hornbeck has a girlfriend? A girlfriend he hugs and kisses? He's only eight years old."

"They're making third graders different these days," I said.

"No kidding. Who's your girlfriend?" Stacey asked Hornbeck.

"Nicole Olsen."

"Nicole Olsen?" Stacey thought outloud. "Michelle's sister? Is she the little girl who always has . . . ?" She pointed to her nose.

"That's right. Nicole is the kid with the runny nose," I said.

"Nicole's kisses taste funny," Hornbeck said.

"Yuck." Stacey squirmed. "That's disgusting."

My brother flopped in front of the TV. "Can I watch with you?"

"Actually, you can watch whatever you want, Hornbeck," I picked my grandmother's camcorder off the side table. "We're done here. Stacey and I are going to make our own show. Stacey is going to say something to Mom and Dad."

My folks are weather scientists. They're in Antarctica for a couple of years doing research on ozone holes and ice and weather stuff. While they're away, Hornbeck and I are staying with our grandmother in Pirate Cove, Maine. Gram owns a bed and breakfast guest house called Bed & Roses.

Once a month, Mom and Dad send us a videotape shot around the U.S. research station at the South Pole. We do the same, filming stuff we're doing in Pirate Cove.

This month I thought I'd introduce the folks to my friends. So I invited some of my eighth grade classmates over to Bed & Roses to appear on camera.

"Show Stacey what you've shot already, Garret," Hornbeck said. "Show her what Butcher and Baker did. It's funny."

"Okay." I ejected the mini-tape from the camcorder and tossed it to my brother. Hornbeck slipped it into the VHS cassette and fed the VCR.

The tape rolled and I appeared on the TV screen, sitting on the foot of my bed. I'd turned the camera on *auto* and set it on the edge of my

4

dresser. "Hi, Mom and Dad, I hope you're staying warm. This month I'm going to introduce you to some of my friends. But before I start, I want to show you my new room. You might recognize it as Third Floor Back."

Third Floor Back used to be the smallest of the four guest rooms in Bed & Roses.

"I'm here in Third Floor Back because Gram said it's my room until you come back. Sharing the downstairs bedroom with Hornbeck was like living in a sardine can."

"I know the feeling," Stacey said. "I shared the guest room in my uncle's house with my brother until we moved into our place. Nearly a whole month with my brother, Travis, snoring in the next bed. It was horrible."

Hornbeck propped himself on his elbows. "We should have traded, Stacey," he said. "Travis could have stayed here with me and Garrett could have stayed with you."

Stacey blushed.

On the TV, I spoke to my parents, telling them about my marks at school, how I'd made the junior high floor hockey team, how I planned to try out for the basketball team. After a minute, the doorbell rang on the tape and I grinned into the lens. "That should be Delton," I said as I hopped off the bed and switched off the camcorder.

In real life it took ten minutes to get Delton set

up in the kitchen; on the tape it was a fraction of a second of on, off, on again. Delton appeared on the TV, leaning against the kitchen table. My voice could be heard off-camera.

"Like I said, Mom and Dad, I want you to meet some of my buddies. This is my best friend, Delton. Delton is a great fisherman. He's also very superstitious."

Delton frowned. "That's not true. I'm a *little* superstitious. I'm not as bad as I used to be. I don't wear a rabbit's foot anymore. I don't look for four-leaf clovers. I don't . . ."

At that moment, Midnight, one of Gram's cats, slipped through the pet flap in the back door. Delton always checks to make sure Midnight is out of the house before he comes in. That's because Midnight's fur is completely black.

Delton froze in mid-sentence and his eyes bulged white. "I, um . . . I . . . that's Midnight. I've got to go now." He turned around and tried to leave the kitchen as fast as possible. Unfortunately, he forgot where he was leaning. He hit the pointed corner of our kitchen table at tummy level. Instantly, he dropped to his knees.

At that point, I'd switched off the camera to help my friend.

"Ow! That must have hurt," Stacey said. "Is he all right?"

"He's fine. But believe it or not Delton was so

6

spooked by Midnight, he crawled out the front door."

Francine Buford's face appeared on the TV.

"This is really funny," Hornbeck announced.

"Greetings, parental units of Garrett." My classmate Francine grinned on the TV screen. "Your son has asked me to tell you something about myself. Well, I'm going to tell you something even he doesn't know. I do great imitations. Not of people. Of things. The first one I want to do is one I learned on vacation when I was in the first grade. This is an airplane toilet flushing."

Francine pinched her nostrils half-shut and blew out a forceful snort.

Hornbeck had a fit.

"Next," Francine went on, "I'd like to do the sound a bullfrog makes when you sit on it." She proceeded to swallow three gulps of air and exploded with the loudest burp I've ever heard. It fuzzed the TV speakers.

After Francine completed her imitations of a hippo with hiccups and a raptor with a cold, there was a brief flash of static. The picture resolved outside of Bed & Roses and Delton's image reappeared.

"Hi, Mr. and Mrs. Hawgood." He rubbed his gut. "I feel much better now. I came back to try again. Okay, I admit it. I'm *very* superstitious. I also like to fish. That's enough about me. I want to tell you how your oldest son made me laugh on Tuesday. In fact, he made most of the students in Bay of Bays laugh, too."

"My folks don't want to hear about that," my cautious voice spoke from behind the camera.

Delton winked into the lens. "Sure they do. They want to know why your nickname is 'Oscar' in Bay of Bays. After all, it was your parents' gift everyone laughed about."

My sigh could be heard on the tape. "Okay, tell away."

Delton grinned. "The first game of the boys' floor hockey season was on Tuesday afternoon in Bay of Bays. When we got there, Garrett found out he'd forgot his shorts. The only person with an extra pair was Butcher, and Butcher is twice as big as Garrett. On the first shift, Garrett gets a breakaway, goes charging toward their net and right in the middle of the charge, his shorts drop down to his ankles."

You could hear me sigh again.

"Garrett did a face plant on the Bay of Bays gym floor. There he was lying on the floor, with just about the entire school watching, and what does everyone see? Yellow boxers with Oscar The Grouch on them. Pretty soon there's a hundred and fifty people busting a gut. Then, as Garrett stands up and pulls up his shorts, everyone

8

starts chanting, 'Oscar! Oscar!' It was such a hoot."

"I feel embarrassed all over again," my voice said. "You've told my parents about my embarrassment. Are you happy now?"

Delton bobbed his head. "Yeah."

"Good," my voice said. "Because I think I see Midnight by the . . ." I didn't even finish the sentence before my buddy was running away as fast as he could.

Hornbeck pressed the *pause* button. "I have to go to the bathroom. I'll be right back." My brother ran out of the room as fast as Delton had on the tape.

"Little kids always hold it until the last minute," Stacy said. "Travis is the same way."

"Losing my shorts wasn't *that* funny," I complained.

"Yes, it was," Stacey said. "You were the highlight of the game for the cheerleaders. All the girls thought your underwear was very cute. I'm almost jealous."

"Sometimes I wish my folks had never bought me *Sesame Street* clothes as a joke gift for my birthday."

"Maybe you can explain that," Stacey puzzled. "You told everyone the clothes were a joke, so why were you wearing them to a floor hockey game?"

9

"For good luck. Last summer we lost the first six baseball games of the season. When game seven came, my Oscar boxers were the only ones not in the laundry. So I had to wear them. We won twenty-one to three. So I wore them next game. We won that one fourteen to zip. Every time I wore The Grouch we won. When I didn't, we lost."

"I see." Stacey smiled. "So what were you saying about Delton being too superstitious?" She waited a second and added, "Oscar."

Hornbeck hopped into the room, flopped in front of the TV again and pressed the *play* button. The tape rolled and Stacey's cousins, Butcher Bortowski, and his younger brother, Baker, were standing in our back yard.

"This is even funnier," Hornbeck giggled.

My friend, Butcher, stared at the camera. "So what do you want me to say, Garrett?" he asked.

"Anything," my voice coached from behind the camera.

"Okay, I'm Butcher Bortowski." He looked down at Baker. "This is my dopey brother, Baker."

"I'm not dopey," Baker challenged.

"Yes, you are, twerp."

"You're dopier, Butcher."

"Guys!" I called.

Butcher stared stupidly. "I got nothing to say."

10

"Tell my folks anything," my disembodied voice directed. "Tell them your favorite color. Your favorite food. Your favorite movie. Anything."

Baker, who is in the same class as Hornbeck, waved his thumb in his brother's direction. "I can tell your parents something about Butcher. He eats the lint from the dryer."

Butcher took a lazy swing at the little guy and Baker hopped out of the way. "I only ate lint once," Butcher defended.

"When you were little?" I asked.

"No, last weekend," Baker volunteered. "I caught him by the dryer pulling strips of lint off the filter and shoving them into his mouth."

"You . . . what? Why would you eat lint, Butcher?"

"I wanted to see what it would taste like," the big guy explained.

"Did you like it?"

"No, it's got no taste. But I didn't know that 'til I tried it."

There was disbelief in my taped voice. "Fascinating, Butcher."

"Why don't we show them how we play 'Bill And Ben, the Trash Can Men'?" Baker suggested.

Butcher scratched his head. "Yeah? You think your parents would like to see that, Garrett?"

"Whatever 'Bill And Ben, the Trash Can Men' is, I'm sure they'd love to see it. They're living

11

under a dome at the coldest place on the planet. I have a feeling anything is going to interest them."

"Okay," Butcher said. "Where are your trash cans?"

The camera followed them as Butcher removed the green garbage bag from our beat-up metal trash can and Baker dumped the soda cans out of the big, plastic recycling can. They returned in front of me and flipped the trash cans over their heads.

Stacey and I joined Hornbeck in laughter. It was so funny. Butcher stood with his legs sticking out of an upside-down garbage can. Baker was even funnier. Only his black Reeboks could be seen under the can.

The two Bortowski brothers then began a hilarious dance on our back lawn, bouncing into and off each other. Stacey laughed so hard her face turned crimson red. I laughed harder because I knew what was coming next.

After a minute of crazy prancing on the grass, little Baker tossed aside his trash can, ran over to Gram's vegetable garden and grabbed a small shovel. He charged back to his brother, wound back and took a grand slam swing at Butcher. The air shuddered with a deafening BONG when the head of the shovel added another dimple to the already-dented metal.

"Ow!" Stacey exclaimed.

Hornbeck howled with delight.

Baker dropped Gram's shovel and darted out of the picture.

Butcher threw off the metal trash can and snapped his head from side to side, searching for his brother. "Where is the little creep?"

"Are you okay?" I asked from behind the camera.

"What's today?" Butcher puzzled. "Why are you asking that? It's Saturday. You should know that."

"I didn't ask what day it was."

"Huh? What are you saying, Hawgood?" He put his index fingers into his ears and wiggled them. "I got this buzzing noise in my ears. Where's my jerk brother?"

"He beat it down Shore Road."

"What? He went to eat a raw toad?"

"Do you hurt?" I asked.

He shook his head. "No, I don't have a skirt. What a dumb thing to ask. Where's Baker?"

"If you can't hear, maybe you should see Doc Jenkins."

"What? He went to sneer at hot penguins? You sure are talking stupid, Garrett." With that comment, Butcher booted across our back yard and down the street, searching for his brother.

Our TV screen dissolved into snow. "That's all

13

I have so far. Turn it off, and give me the camcorder tape back, Hornbeck."

Still laughing, my brother shut down the VCR.

"That was so bizarre," Stacey said. "Did Butcher catch Baker?"

"Not as far as I know." I held up the camcorder. "You ready to do your bit, Stacey?"

"I guess so. I sure hope your parents like me."

"Hey, they're going to think you're something else."

Her features dissolved again.

Joe Smooth just got smoother, I thought.

We exited Bed & Roses with Hornbeck on our heels and discovered Stacey's brother trotting up the front walk wearing a wide, mischievous grin. It took me a couple of seconds to realize something about Travis wasn't right.

Something was very, very wrong.

**"H**i, everyone," Travis called. "What do you think? Do I look cool?"

"You look funny," Hornbeck said.

And he did. Stacey's brother had a chest.

Travis patted his chest. "It's Halloween in two weeks. I want to go out as a woman this year. So I stuffed a pair of socks in a bra. Then I thought it looked so funny I came over to show Hornbeck. Neat, huh?"

"It's a hoot," Hornbeck told his friend.

"You certainly look different," I told him.

"When I was walking past the cafe, Old Lady Dawson came out," Travis said. "When she saw me, she almost fainted."

Hornbeck laughed. "You scared our teacher?"

"Yeah." Travis grinned. "She got all shaky."

Hornbeck laughed harder. "Where did you get the bra, Travis?"

"From my sister's underwear drawer," he answered.

Stacey took a step toward her brother and planted her fists on her hips. "What? You went into my room without asking?"

"Yeah."

"You went searching through my dresser without my permission?"

"Yeah."

"How could you?" she shouted. "How many times have I told you to leave my things alone?"

Travis shrugged. "A couple of hundred. But I like bugging you."

Stacey stomped a foot in frustration. "Sometimes I hate you."

"How can you hate your brother?" Travis taunted. "I'm so cute and cuddly."

"Ewww!" Stacey spat. Then, "Wait a sec. You were in my underwear drawer? You didn't take anything else, did you?"

He slowly shook his head. "Not really. Just your dopey diary."

"You took my diary?"

Travis grinned at me. "There's all kinds of mushy stuff about you in it, Garrett. Give me twenty bucks and I'll let you read it."

"Don't you dare!" Stacey threatened.

16

Travis was acting brave because he knew his sister. No matter how angry she got, it just wasn't in Stacey to take a swipe at the brat. Well, there was no rule which said I couldn't do something.

I placed the camcorder on the grass, grabbed the shoulder of Travis's sweat shirt and yanked him toward Stacey. Then I reached under the back of his shorts and grabbed the elastic waistband of his underwear.

"Hey, what are you doing?" he protested. "Let me go, Garrett." He tried to wriggle free and I tightened my grip on his Jockeys to hold him in place.

I looked at Stacey. "Do you want me to give him a major wedgie?"

"I just want him to stop going into my room," she answered. "And I want my diary back."

"I don't know, Stacey. I think he needs to be taught a lesson. I think he deserves the mother of all wedgies."

"Big kids are not supposed to pick on little kids," Travis whined. "There's laws against it."

"Listen, Travis," I said in my toughest voice. "Stop being a doofus. Respect your sister's privacy. If I hear you've been in her stuff again, I'm going to be upset and you don't want to upset me. Understand?"

"I thought you were a nice guy," he complained.

"I am. And I want you to be a nice guy, too. When Stacey gets home, her diary better be back where it belongs." I gave his underwear elastic a gentle tug. "I'm counting on your cooperation, Travis."

"Ow," he grumbled. "That hurts."

"Not yet it doesn't," I threatened.

"Geez, just because you're Stacey's boyfriend doesn't mean you're my big brother." He looked at Hornbeck. "Let's go, Hornbeck. There's too many donkeys around here."

The little guys trucked across the grass and down the sidewalk.

"Hey, Travis," I called.

They turned.

"Put the diary back first," I ordered.

"Yes, sir." Travis mocked a salute and he and Hornbeck headed down Shore Road.

"Thanks, Garrett," Stacey smiled, soft and cute-like. "Could I ask you to do something else for me? Another favor?"

"Sure, what are friends for?"

"Travis needs someone to have that private talk with. Will you do it?"

"*That* private talk?"

"He needs someone to tell him the facts of life."

"The facts of life?"

"You know."

"I do?"

"The facts of life. Travis needs somebody to tell him about the differences between boys and girls. About growing up. The birds and the bees. The private stuff."

"The birds and the bees? Private stuff? He's only a little kid. Why does he need to know anything about that?"

"Because he's asking about it. I read somewhere that parents should always answer their children's questions about anything, no matter what age they are."

I thought about that. "That may be true, Stacey. But last time I checked, I'm not Travis's father. Why doesn't your dad talk to him?"

"Dad?" she scoffed. "When it comes to talking about stuff like that, he gets all embarrassed. He gave me a book, if you can believe it."

"What about you, then? You're his sister."

"I'm a girl. Travis doesn't want to hear private things from a girl."

"All I know is what I learned in sixth grade Health class."

"That's enough to answer my brother's questions," she reasoned. "Will you talk to him?"

"I guess," I mumbled.

She squeezed my hand. "Thanks. You're the best boyfriend I've ever had."

"I thought you said I'm the *first* boyfriend you've ever had."

She winked. "That's right. And you're the best so far." She paused. "Garrett, do you like Francine?"

I nodded. "She's cool."

"I mean, do you like her in the same way you like me?"

"No. Why?"

"Well, you asked her to make the tape to your folks before you asked me."

"No, I didn't. I knew you were coming over this afternoon. I knew we could do your bit now. Francie came over last night because she's going shopping in Bay of Bays today."

Stacey smiled. "I'm so lucky to know you, Garrett."

And I'm so lucky Stacey moved to Pirate Cove six weeks ago, I thought.

I remembered the moment I first saw her. Mr. Nightingale, the assistant principal, was introducing her to the class. I took a look and thought Stacey's long, straight hair, piercing green eyes, and lopsided smile redefined the meaning of cute. Add to that her Apache headband, poet blouse and floor length flowered dress, and I was looking at someone who almost made it hard to breathe. I knew I was hooked.

"You know, I'd be really hurt if you liked a girl in the same way you liked me."

"No chance of that," I assured her.

20

"I'd be even more hurt if you kissy-faced with another girl."

I laughed. "Give me a break."

Stacey looked at her watch. "It's my turn to make supper tonight. I have to go in a few minutes."

"Sure thing." I reached down, picked up the camcorder, pressed the *on* button and focused on her face. "Say 'hi' to my folks first."

"What? Just like that?" she said, surprised. "I haven't thought about what I want to say."

"I'll introduce you while you're thinking. Okay, Mom and Dad, here she is. Stacey, my girlfriend. She's going to tell you all about herself."

"That's not an introduction. You didn't give me time to think of anything."

"The tape is rolling."

She sighed. "Hello, Mr. and Mrs. Hawgood. I feel like I know you already, even though we've never met. Garrett has shown me pictures of you and told me all kinds of things you did when you were living in Vancouver. I'm a Scorpio. I'm really into horoscopes and, even though Garrett is an Aries and Aries and Scorpios aren't supposed to get along, I did his personal horoscope and he has Scorpio in his Romance House, so I guess that's why we get along so well."

"I have the feeling my folks have no idea what you're talking about," I said.

I noticed Travis—minus his Halloween ex-
tras—and Hornbeck in the viewfinder. They'd returned to Bed & Roses and stood on the sidewalk,
watching us. Little Baker Bortowski was with
them.

"Last year I lived in Orlando," Stacey continued. "Which was okay, but I like Pirate Cove so
much better because . . ."

Travis whispered something into my brother's
ear. Hornbeck nodded and smiled. Travis did the
same to Baker. Baker imitated Hornbeck. Then,
in a surprisingly coordinated fashion, the three
kids lifted their T-shirts over their bellies.

And I couldn't help but laugh at what I saw.

Stacey stopped listing the reasons why she
liked Pirate Cove. "What? Why are you laughing?
Did I say something funny?"

The three little guys had drawn happy faces
on their stomachs with a felt pen. One of the eyes
of the happy face was their belly buttons, so it
looked like the faces were all winking. Above
Travis's happy face was the word *Stacey*. Above
Hornbeck's was *Looks*. Above Baker's was the
word *Funny*. I zoomed the lens on Travis's bare
tummy. My folks would get a mega-chuckle out
of this.

"Why are you laughing?" Stacey asked.

I pointed in the direction of the sidewalk and

Stacey turned around. Three naked felt-penned third grade stomachs greeted her.

"Of all the . . ." she said.

As if they'd rehearsed it, the boys pulled down their T-shirts in sync and vanished down the road.

"That was so childish," Stacey groaned.

I switched off the camcorder. "It was funny, too."

"Boys! I don't think I'll ever understand boys. Why do you think stuff like that is funny?"

I shrugged. "It just is."

"I bet you even think The Three Stooges are funny, don't you?"

"Of course. Doesn't everyone?"

"Boys," Stacey repeated. "I'm glad I wasn't born one." She glanced at her watch again. "I have to go make supper now. I'll do the video to your parents tomorrow, okay?"

"No problem. I have to go tidy up the rooms for our mystery guests anyway."

"Give me a call when you know who they are, Garrett." Stacey disappeared in the same direction as the boys.

I walked into Bed & Roses, put the camcorder on the hall table, and went upstairs to tidy up the guest rooms for the mystery people. To my pleasant surprise, I discovered Gram had already done everything.

23

While checking the guest bathroom I noticed a copy of *People* magazine in the magazine rack next to the toilet. Leighla Livingston was on the cover. So I sat on the edge of the tub to read about her.

The article on Leighla said she wasn't the youngest supermodel ever—that a lot of thirteen-year-olds had become big-time models ever since Brooke Shields became famous when she was only eleven. It went on to say how tough Leighla's life was, how all she did was work, how she needed a bodyguard and was hounded by guys who take photos of famous people for supermarket tabloids.

Real tough, I thought. I'd trade life in Pirate Cove to be rich and famous like Leighla.

What should I do now? I thought. There was still an hour until supper. That meant there was plenty of time for a nap. I returned the magazine to the rack and went to my room. I kicked off my sneakers, dropped onto my bed, buried my head in my pillow, closed my eyes and pictured my favorite fantasy.

In my fantasy a girl and I are trapped in an igloo by a raging Arctic blizzard. That afternoon I imagined the girl was Stacey.

*"Oh, Garrett," Stacey says in my imagination. "I'm so frightened."*

24

*"There's no problem,"* I assure her. *"The blizzard will be over in a week or two."*

*"Whatever are we going to do all that time?" Stacey wonders.*

*"We'll think of something,"* I answer.

*"It's so cold in here."* Stacey shivers.

*"Then I guess the first thing we should do is cuddle to stay warm. You know, hug and stuff."*

*"Okay,"* she agrees. *"I'd like to kissy-face."*

I slipped into a spongy half-consciousness. The pillow was perfectly molded to my head and I was so pleasantly relaxed, I drifted into sleep. And I dreamed.

In my dream, I was lying on my bed, napping, just at the point of falling into a complete sleep when the strangest feeling showered over me. It wasn't startling and it wasn't frightening. It was just a feeling. I felt I wasn't alone in Third Floor Back.

*Felt* may be the wrong word. Perhaps *sensed* is better. I sensed there was somebody else in my room. I wasn't scared. And I didn't wake up. Slowly, I lifted my head a couple of inches off the pillow, opened my eyes a fraction and squinted into the room.

And there, at the foot of my bed, was a girl.

In my dream, there was no surprise, no fear. Only curiosity.

The girl was a sharp image against an indistinct, blurry background. She was ten years old—maybe eleven—with coal black hair. Her bangs were clipped sharply at eyebrow level; the rest of her hair hung straight past her shoulders. She appeared to be wearing what I thought was a white blouse with baggy, lacy sleeves.

Her eyes, dark and piercing, stared into my face, intense but not threatening.

Every so often, I find myself dreaming and I know I'm dreaming. I really like those times because I can control what's going to happen next. And that's kind of how I felt looking at the girl. There was nothing unusual about her being there. I was merely watching a dream. *Who are you?* I said in my thoughts.

The girl smiled—friendly. She lifted her fingers until they were a fraction of an inch from her lips. The oversized sleeves of her blouse hung loosely in the air. She waved her fingers towards her mouth as if she was trying to say something.

"*What?*" I mumbled.

She gently danced her fingers around her mouth.

"*What? What are you trying to say?*"

An expression of frustration hardened her features.

"*Do you need some help?*" I asked.

Knock! Knock! "Garrett!"

I heard the door open and suddenly I was awake. Hornbeck was shaking my shoulder.

"Get up, Garrett," Hornbeck panted. "You've got to see this. You're not going to believe it."

27

# chapter 3

I lifted myself so I was resting on my elbows and looked at the foot of the bed. Of course, the girl wasn't there. "Wow," I said to Hornbeck. "I just had the weirdest dream. I dreamed there was a girl at the foot of the bed. She was pointing to her lips and . . ."

"Forget your dream, Garrett!" Hornbeck ordered. "Come look at this! It's awesome."

I swung my feet over the side of the bed so I was sitting up and fully awake. I rubbed my eyes and stretched. "What? Look at what? What's going on, Hornbeck?"

"Out back," he said. "In the driveway." He scooted out of the room and I heard his sneakers thump down the stairs. The back screen door slammed as he ran outside. I followed my brother and found him on the back stoop, staring at the driveway with wide, disbelieving eyes. "Have you ever seen anything like that before?" he whispered.

"Only in movies," I answered.

Parked behind Bed & Roses was an impressive stretch limousine, shiny and black, long and definitely expensive-looking. It was parked in a spot where it was hidden from Shore Road by our house. Someone passing by wouldn't be able to see it from the front.

"I've never, ever seen a car like that," Hornbeck said. "It must cost a million bucks."

"It's got to be our mystery guests," I figured. "This is the first time someone has ever arrived at Bed and Roses in a limo. I wonder who it is."

Gram was already standing on the driveway, wearing her welcome smile, ready to greet whoever was inside. The driver's door swung open and a large, muscular man in sunglasses, wearing a classy-looking gray business suit, got out.

"Welcome to Bed and Roses," Gram said.

The guy ignored her and examined our yard and driveway, slowly turning his head left, then right, then left again, like Arnold Schwarzenegger playing the killer robot in *The Terminator* movies.

Hornbeck and I walked down the path. We stopped beside Gram.

"Welcome to Bed and Roses," my grandmother

repeated. "I'm sure you're going to have a pleasant stay."

The man grunted a response and continued to eyeball the yard. I peered into the darkened windows of the limo. They were so black there was no way you could see anything. Whoever was inside was still a mystery.

"Is there a reason you're not speaking to me?" Gram asked. "Do you speak English?"

The man tilted his head and held his gaze on her for an uncomfortable few seconds. Finally he said, "It is as you said. No one can see into your back yard."

"And I'm pleased to meet you too," Gram said, a little sarcastically. "My name is Estelle LaBlanc and I'm the owner of Bed and Roses. I will do everything I can to make your stay with us as pleasant as possible."

He glanced at the outside of Bed & Roses. "I'm sure we will enjoy ourselves in your establishment. You may call me Karl." There was a hint of an accent, maybe German, maybe some eastern European place.

"That's Mr. Karl. . . ?" Gram probed. "Your last name is. . . ?"

"Karl is all you need to know," he said with authority. Karl's head rotated until the sunglasses faced me. Then he studied Hornbeck for a moment. "Who are these children?"

"With all respect, I'm not a child, sir," I said. "I'm in the eighth grade. Miss Scott, my Homeroom teacher, says eighth graders are young adults."

"Garret, let's not get into that," Gram said. Then she introduced us to Karl.

Karl glared at me and stroked his chin. "Ah, yes, Garrett Hawgood. I have something for you."

Something for me? Weird. "What is it, sir?"

"You do not need to know at this moment," he said firmly. "I will let you have it once we are inside the house."

"Mr. Polite," I whispered to myself.

Gram heard me and shot a disapproving glance. "No more comments like that," she scolded. "These people are our guests. And this is obviously a special circumstance. We shouldn't judge before we find out exactly what is going on. Perhaps there is a reason for this gentleman's rudeness."

Way to go, Gram, I thought. Make it sound polite, but let the guy know you think he's a jerk.

Karl missed the put-down. "Is that your garage over there?" he asked.

"Yes, it is," Gram answered. "And like I said to the person on the phone, you're welcome to park your car inside so no one will see it. Although I do find it a little odd."

Karl arched an eyebrow. "Odd?"

31

"Why you would want to keep such a big automobile a secret when you've just driven it through town," Gram explained.

I thought I caught a hint of a pleased smile around Karl's mouth. "We came into town on the Old Mill Road. Nobody saw us."

"The Old Mill Road?" Gram said. "I thought only Pirate Cove residents knew The Old Mill Road route to the interstate."

"I make it my business to know everything," Karl declared. "I will feel better when the car is in your garage." He twisted and nodded once at the darkened windows of the limousine. The rear door swung open and a tall, thin woman stepped out. She, too, was dressed in a gray business-type suit and wore the same sunglasses as the huge guy.

This is getting weirder, I thought.

The woman checked out our yard the same way Karl had. Then she leaned into the open car door. "All right," she said to someone inside. "The area is clear. Everything seems safe."

Safe, I thought. You're in Pirate Cove. This has got to be one of the safest places in America.

Instantly, a smaller third figure emerged. I had no idea if it was a man or a woman because the person was covered from head to knees in a gray blanket. All I could see were the legs of blue jeans and white sneakers.

32

The woman grabbed an elbow of the draped figure and directed the person up our back steps. Karl followed close behind, doing his imitation of a killer robot from the future. Hornbeck, Gram and I glanced at each other and trailed the puzzling group into Bed & Roses.

Once inside, the woman said to Gram, "Show us the rooms, please."

The man pointed at us. "And I will need to speak to the boys in a minute." He looked directly at my brother and me. "Please do not leave the building until I talk to you."

"Yes, sir," Hornbeck replied meekly.

Hornbeck and I waited in the living room while Gram escorted the woman and the carpet person upstairs. Karl went outside to hide the limo in our garage.

My brother and I sat on the couch.

"Who the heck is under the blanket?" I puzzled.

"I don't like the driver," Hornbeck said. "He's scary. He's big enough to be a wrestler."

"He's not just a limo driver," I pointed out. "Karl's the bodyguard for the person under the blanket."

"I don't like the woman either," Hornbeck whined. "She reminds me of that witch in *The Wizard of Oz*."

Two minutes later, Karl returned and went upstairs carrying several suitcases. "It's got to be somebody important," I said. "Why would they come to Pirate Cove? To Bed and Roses?"

When Gram and Karl came back down the stairs a few minutes after that, I noticed my grandmother was smiling, and our guest's frown was slightly softer.

"Again, I apologize for being so harsh outside," Karl said to Gram. "I hope you understand now."

"I suppose I do," she replied as they entered the room. Gram looked at Hornbeck and me. "Boys, the gentleman has something important to say to you." She returned her attention to Karl. "I'll just go start dinner." Then she left us alone with him.

Karl sat in a chair, facing us. "I'll be brief." His voice was stern. "You cannot tell anyone who is staying in your house. None of your friends can know. It must be kept a secret. The press must not find out she is staying here."

She, I thought.

"You will not tell anyone. Is that understood?"

"Yes, sir," Hornbeck said nervously.

"I guess," I mumbled.

"Do not guess," Karl ordered. "Be sure. It is important the paparazzi do not discover her location."

"The pepperoni?" Hornbeck asked.

"Paparazzi," I told him. "That's what they call the photographers who take pictures of famous

34

people when those people don't want their photos taken. I read about them in a *People* story on Leighla Livingston."

Karl stiffened, as if he was startled.

"What's wrong?" I asked him. "That's right, isn't it? That's what those guys are called?"

Karl got himself back under control. "I was surprised when you said the name of the person upstairs."

"Leighla Livingston?" The words caught in my throat.

"Leighla Livingston," Hornbeck said. "She's the pretty girl in the TV commercials. Great, the pretty girl is staying with us."

Leighla Livingston!

I couldn't believe my younger brother was sitting next to me, so calm, as if having Leighla Livingston in our house was a normal, everyday event.

Why wasn't he speechless?

Like me.

The person Delton thought was the best-looking girl in the whole world was staying in our bed and breakfast. It was incredible. I forced myself to take a deep breath. "Leighla Livingston?" I squeaked.

Karl nodded and reached into the inside pocket of his suit jacket and pulled out a letter-sized envelope. "Miss Livingston's aunt recommended your establishment as a place where she could spend a few days of peace and quiet." He handed the envelope to me. "This is from Miss Livingston's aunt. She asked me to make sure you read it after we'd checked in. Please read it now." It was more a command than a request.

I ripped open the envelope, pulled out a sheet of note paper and read the handwritten message.

*Hi Garrett—*
*It's me, Lisa Liddle. How are you doing? I can't wait to visit Bed & Roses again. I'm in the middle of shooting the new movie. Things are going really well. We're way under budget. Not that you're interested in budgets, of course. But it's good news for us.*

"It's from Lisa Liddle," I told Hornbeck. Then to Karl, "Lisa Liddle is the big movie star."
Karl nodded. "I am aware of that fact."
"She comes and stays with us when she's learning her lines," I went on. "She says the peace and quiet of Pirate Cove helps her get into her new roles."
Karl nodded at my comment.
I read on.

*I'm writing to introduce you to my niece Leighla. You've probably seen her on TV or in magazines. It seems her face is everywhere these days. My brother, Douglas (Leighla's dad) told me a few weeks ago how tired Leighla is. My niece works very hard and doesn't have any time for herself. She's also bothered by photographers and reporters. I told her to take a vacation to Bed & Roses to get away from everything. I told her your town does wonders for me.*

*One of the main reasons I recommended Pirate Cove is because I knew you'd be there to welcome her. I hope this doesn't sound like an unusual request, Garrett, but would you become her friend? She's around adults all day and her mother thinks she needs somebody her own age to talk to. She needs to be a normal, average thirteen-year-old for a few days. Maybe you can take her to Hole's Island.*

*Thanks.*

*Say hello to your grandmother and Hornbeck for me.*

Lisa L.

Karl regarded me curiously. I guessed he didn't know what was in the note. For some reason, I felt I had to share it with him. I passed the letter into his large hand. "Ms. Liddle wants me to become Leighla's friend, sir."

Karl scanned the writing and nodded his head once. "That will be satisfactory." He handed the note back to me. "You will become friends with Miss Livingston." It was more like a command than a statement.

Become friends with Leighla Livingston? I thought. Why did I feel suddenly afraid? I slipped the letter into the back pocket of my jeans. "I'm not sure," I mumbled at Karl. "I mean, Leighla Livingston? I wouldn't have a clue what to say to her. She's famous. I'm just a regular eighth grader in a small town. She's *the* Leighla Livingston."

"She just needs to relax," Karl said. "You will help her relax."

"I'll . . . what? Help her relax. I can't do this, sir."

"Maybe you could give her a message," Hornbeck suggested.

"A what?"

"A message. Like they do for Gram's back in the clinic in Bay of Bays."

"That's a massage."

"Oh," Hornbeck said. "Gram always says she feels relaxed after she has a massage."

"I'm not going to massage Leighla Livingston," I said. Although for some reason, the thought wasn't exactly unpleasant.

"Under no circumstances will you touch Miss Livingston," Karl warned.

"I don't want to touch anyone," I protested. "It's just that I don't think I can be Leighla's friend."

As if on cue, Leighla bounced down the stairs, dressed in a white t-shirt and blue jeans, with a fanny pack on her hip, and flashing her famous off-center smile and sparkling green eyes.

chapter 4

As soon as Leighla entered the sitting room, we all stood up.

"This place is wonderful, Karl," she exclaimed. "It's even better than I thought it would be. My room is so cozy." She turned her attention to Hornbeck and me. "Hi, there. I'm Leighla."

A wave of whatever perfume she was wearing washed around me.

Hornbeck returned her smile. "My name is Hornbeck."

"Hornbeck? That's your real name?"

"You think it's stupid?" Hornbeck asked.

"Of course, I don't," she said. "But it's different. I don't think I've met anyone called Hornbeck before."

Lots of people in my class think it's a dumb name," Hornbeck told her. "My mom named me after a guy in a poem. A captain of a ship."

"It's a great name," Leighla beamed. "It suits you."

My brother grinned. "Thanks. You're real pretty on TV."

She winked at him. "Why, thank you. And may I say you're very handsome."

Hornbeck giggled. "You're pretty on TV, but you're prettier in real life."

That made Leighla laugh. Her laugh was the same as Stacey's, soft and cute. She looked at me. "Are you Hornbeck's brother?"

What I wanted to say was, "Yes, I'm Garrett." But I was so stunned that Leighla Livingston was standing in front of me, smiling, in my living room, wearing some kind of wonderful perfume, with her thumbs casually hooked through the front belt loops of her jeans, that when I opened my mouth, I blurted, "Yeath, my nam is car rat."

"Car rat?" Leighla asked.

"Car rat?" Hornbeck echoed. "When did you change your name to Car rat?"

Leighla is so good-looking, I thought. She was even more good-looking than Stacey. I did a quick second think. Nobody is as good-looking as Stacey. Nobody real that is. The only girls better-looking are on TV or movies or in ads. And everyone knows they use makeup and fake photography. Tricks. They play around with lights, and color over their pimples and moles. Nobody looks as good as those people. But they aren't real, not real like Stacey.

I checked out Leighla's soft green eyes and tiny nose. Her shining hair. Lopsided smile. Here was one of those unreal people standing less than six feet away from me.

So much for the Trick Photography Theory, I said to myself.

Here was Leighla Livingston in person looking more wonderful than on TV or in any magazine.

"I'm nut Car rat." My mouth was still full of marbles. "I'm Car rat."

Perplexed, Leighla scrunched up her face. "I'm sorry, but I don't think I understand."

Come on, Bozo, I thought. Get yourself together. Do you want Leighla to think you're the son of Tarzan? I concentrated on producing intelligent speech. "Garrett," I managed to say, nearly normal. "My name's Garrett."

She reached out her hand. "Oh, I wondered if it was you. My Auntie Lisa has told me all about you, Garrett."

I shook hands with the number one young supermodel in the world. Once more, I lost my ability to speak.

Fortunately, I didn't have to because Karl loosened his tie and said, "Remember, Miss Livingston, under no circumstances are you to leave the inn without my permission. That is completely understood?"

"I'm not going anywhere, Karl," she replied.

"With all due respect, Miss Livingston," Karl continued. "That's what you said to me when we were in Miami last week and you went for a walk along the beach."

"I thought the beach was empty," she explained. "And I didn't go far from the hotel."

He eyed her suspiciously.

"I wouldn't have gone if I knew Dennis Fitzgerald was waiting behind the palm trees."

"Who's Dennis Fitzgerald?" Hornbeck asked.

"He is a photographer for United Photo International," Karl said. "His assignment is to follow and photograph Miss Livingston everywhere. We took great precautions to make sure he did not follow us here."

"I've learned my lesson, Karl," Leighla insisted. "I'm not going to go anywhere alone."

Karl acknowledged her with a curt nod and loosened his tie some more. "I am going to change my clothes. I will be in my room if you have need of me." With heavy footsteps, he thundered into the hall and up the stairs. We heard the door to Second Floor Front close.

"He scares me," Hornbeck said.

"Oh, Karl just talks tough," Leighla told my

43

brother. "Underneath, I have the feeling he's really a nice person. He just gets into his job."

"Who's the witch lady?" Hornbeck wanted to know.

Leighla let loose a wonderful laugh. "That's Jennifer. She's from my modeling agency. She's my on-the-road escort, chaperone, manager, teacher and substitute mother. And you're right, she can be a witch at times."

Hornbeck held up his right hand and crossed his heart with his left. "I won't tell anybody you're here," he promised Leighla. Then to me, "I'm going to the kitchen to see how long supper is going to be." Which left Leighla and me alone in the living room.

A sudden breeze billowed the lace curtains and blew Leighla's perfume across the room. She even smells great, I thought.

"So what do you want to do now, Garrett?" Leighla asked.

"Do? Me? You? Huh?"

"Do you want to do something with me?" Leighla asked. "You know, hang around together for a bit?"

I have no idea why I said what I said next. Maybe it was because I was so stunned. My mouth formed the words in my head. "You smell," I declared.

"Pardon?"

"You smell."

She looked hurt. "I smell?"

I tried to recover. "No, no, I don't mean you *stink* smell. Whatever perfume you're wearing stinks nice. I mean it smells nice."

"It's called Minx," she told me. "I get paid to wear it."

"You get paid to wear perfume? Incredible."

"I hate it. I don't like wearing perfume. It smells so phony. My Auntie Lisa thinks I'm too young to wear it. Do you think thirteen is too young to wear perfume? I mean, how many girls in your class use perfume?"

"A couple maybe."

"I have contracts with all kinds of different companies. I get paid to wear one type of jeans. Drink one kind of soda. Eat one kind of cheeseburger. Only brush my teeth with one brand of toothpaste, if you can believe it."

"Wow, really? You get paid to brush your teeth. What a great life."

She sighed. "You think so?" She seemed to take a few seconds to think about it. "I guess sometimes my life is wonderful. There are moments when I'm watching TV in my apartment and one of my commercials comes on and I think 'Hey, that's really me.' "

"You have your *own* apartment?"

45

"In midtown Manhattan. Actually, it's my agency's. I share it with Jennifer."

"Cool." I was really impressed. "Your own apartment. Getting paid to drink soda. Awesome."

"Yeah, it's cool. It's awesome. And sometimes it isn't. Sometimes I wish I was back home, just going to school and hanging out with friends."

"You do?" That was like the President saying, 'I'm happy being President but sometimes I wish I worked at Taco Bell.' It didn't make sense.

"Not that I'd have any friends to hang out with anymore," she confessed. "All my old friends back in St. Albert act like I've moved to another planet instead of New York. I guess I have in a way. The only person who still keeps in touch is Tanya. We talk on the phone every Sunday. We've been friends since the first grade, long before the famous thing happened."

"Don't you have any friends in New York?"

"I'm too busy," she explained. "I work on my shoots in the daytime. In the evening, I have to do my school stuff. I have no time to meet people outside of work. Do you know you're the first boy my age I've talked to in months?"

That was a shocker.

The doorbell rang and Leighla jumped. "I guess I should go up to my room," she said cautiously.

I went to the window and glanced at the front

stoop. Butcher stood on the step wiggling his index fingers in his ears. "It's only my friend, Butcher. He's probably come to ask if I've seen his brother, Baker. It'll only take a sec."

"Butcher and Baker?" Stacey wondered. "Do they have a brother called Candlestick-Maker?"

I chuckled. "You know, I've never thought of that before."

I walked into the hallway and opened the front door. And for a moment, I was overcome by the urge to jump up and down, scream and yell, "Hey, Butcher, you'll never guess who is sitting in my living room. When I tell you, you're going to explode into space!"

Fortunately, the urge to scream and shout about Leighla only lasted for a second. I took a deep breath and in my calmest voice, I said, "Hey, Butcher, you looking for Baker?"

"What? I still can't hear all that good, Garrett."

I repeated the question twenty decibels louder.

"Naw," he answered. "I'm going to get my revenge later. If you want to see something funny, drop by my place at eight o'clock. See how I rack Baker. A cool way to use Kool-Aid. You'll think I'm a genius." He rubbed his ears. "I wish the ringing would stop."

"I think you should get the doc to look at you."

"Huh? I should go to the dock to cook a shoe? What are you talking about?"

I was going to say it again but figured we could be there all evening. "What do you want, Butcher?" I asked loudly.

"Well, I was looking for my bro. I thought maybe he was hiding out by the old mill. He likes playing there. So I go check it out. While I was looking, this awesome car cruises by. A black limo. Real long. So I say to myself, 'What would a limo be doing on the old road?' Then I say, 'If anybody knows, Hawgood does.' "

"Me? Why would I?" I fibbed.

"Huh? You have a wooden eye?"

"Why would I?" I shouted.

He nodded. "Because you guys are the only hotel. I thought maybe they were staying here."

"Sorry, all we have is everyday guests."

"What? You have very gray pests?"

"I have to eat supper in a few minutes," I yelled, hoping he'd get the hint and leave.

"Okay. Drop by my place at eight. Watch me doodley-do Baker." Butcher made a move to turn around and suddenly stopped, twitching his nostril as he sniffed the air. "Minx," he said. "I smell Minx."

"Minks? The weasel animals?"

"What? The wheezing cannibals?"

"Minks!" I hollered. "The fur rodents. You smell minks?"

"No, I smell Minx, the perfume. My mother

48

wears it. Someone in your place is wearing Minx."

Again I fought the impulse to blurt out the name of the person who was five steps away. "Oh," I said casually.

"Mom says Leighla Livingston likes it. You know, the model our age."

"Yeah, I know."

"That Leighla is something else, huh? I bet you'd like to meet her, right?"

"I wouldn't mind."

"Wouldn't you go nuts if you could talk to her?"

I told him the truth. "I'd probably say something dumb."

"Would you like to be stuck on a deserted island with Leighla?"

"I've never thought about it."

"I do. When I'm bored. I think about who I'd like to be shipwrecked on an empty island with. You ever do that?"

"An island? No."

"I'll see you later, Garrett," Butcher said.

I closed the door and returned to the living room. Leighla was peeking out from behind the curtains. "So your friend would like to be shipwrecked with me?"

"Alone on an island with Butcher," I mused. "What a scary thought."

Gram entered the living room. "Supper is

ready," she said. "Karl and Jennifer are going to eat in their rooms. But I hope you'll join us, Leighla. I've already set a place for you."

"Wonderful," Leighla said.

So I ate Gram's spaghetti dinner with *the* Leighla Livingston sitting opposite me. I was surprised how easily she'd been accepted as a normal guest by my grandmother and brother. And by me.

During dinner, we talked about everyday stuff. The weather. The new fall TV shows. Chocolate bars. Butcher eating lint. The conversation never got around to the fact that Leighla's face had been on the cover of *Seventeen* and *Bop* and a dozen other magazines; how she was making thousands of dollars a day; how she was so famous she needed a bodyguard.

After dinner, Gram took dessert to Karl and Jennifer's rooms on the second floor. Through a mouthful of peach pie, Hornbeck told Leighla, "I got a girlfriend. Her name is Nicole. We kissy-face. Her kisses taste funny 'cause she has lergies."

"Lergies?"

"Allergies," I explained to Leighla. "And you don't want to know any more."

"The lergies make her nose run all the time," Hornbeck said. "That's why her kisses taste funny."

Leighla thought about it and decided not to finish her peach pie.

"No more gross stuff, Bro," I warned.

"Nicole wants to be a cowboy when she grows up," Hornbeck continued. "Nicole thinks cows are cute. She thinks I'm as cute as a cow." My brother pushed his chair away. "I'm going to see Travis. See you guys later."

Once Hornbeck left, Leighla stood up and began to clear the kitchen table.

"Hey," I protested. "You're not allowed to do that. You're a guest here."

"Don't be silly, Garrett."

So we loaded the dishwasher together.

When we were finished Leighla looked out the side window and took in the scenery. "You're so lucky to live here. Pirate Cove is so pretty."

"I know. Even though I've seen the view every day for a year and a half, I still think it's like living in a postcard."

Leighla pointed across the bay at Hole's Island. "What's that?" she asked. "It looks like an old castle."

"It's what's left of a mansion. No one lives on the island. It's completely deserted. It's Pirate Cove's tourist spot. In the summer we take guests out to Hole's Island to show them around. Your aunt likes going there."

51

Leighla spun around. "You take guests out? How?"

"In our boat. My grandfather bought a Joycraft forty years ago. Joycrafts are to boats what Harleys are to motorcycles. It's named after my grandmother."

"It's called *The Gram?*"

I laughed. "No, it's named *The Estelle*. It runs like new."

"Will your grandfather take me to Hole's Island?"

"Gramps died before I was born. I take the guests over."

"Would you take me over?"

"I guess so. But didn't Karl say you aren't allowed to leave the house?"

She stared out at the island. "He's just worried people will see me. But you said there's no one living out there."

"It's true there's nobody on Hole's Island, but somebody could see you along Shore Road. And a lot of the time there's fishermen on Big Dock. Didn't you promise Karl you wouldn't go outside?"

Leighla grinned mischievously. "No, I promised him I wouldn't go outside alone. Let's go to Hole's Island right now. I'll disguise myself." She unzipped her fanny pack, pulled out a ponytail tie and quickly fixed her hair. Then she removed a pair of sunglasses and slipped them on. "There, I'm disguised."

Now she looked like Leighla Livingston in a ponytail and sunglasses.

"If you want my opinion, you look exactly . . ."

She didn't wait for me to finish. With a casual "Let's go," she marched into the hall and out the front door.

chapter 5

**"W**hat the. . . ?" For a moment I stood there, wondering what I should do. Should I go get Gram? Karl? Jennifer? Who? I thought for a few seconds and then decided I shouldn't tell anyone. Snitching would get Leighla into trouble.

In hindsight, I made an A-plus mistake. Karl and Jennifer were responsible for Leighla's safety. And because Leighla was staying at Bed & Roses, Gram and I were responsible, too. I should have told someone. If I had, the bad stuff that happened wouldn't have happened.

But I didn't fink. Instead, I ran after Leighla and caught up with her at the end of the front path. For some reason, I checked up and down the street the way Karl had, expecting to see . . . who knows what?

"Leighla," I said. It seemed odd to call her name like we were old friends. "I don't think this is such a good idea. Maybe you should get Karl's permission first."

She didn't stop.

"Your disguise isn't . . . well, it isn't all that great. Somebody is going to recognize you. We *do* have cable in Pirate Cove. People buy magazines here. Somebody will know who you are."

She kept walking.

"This is a small town town, Leighla. People will check you out. They'll look at you because they don't know who you are. My Homeroom teacher, Miss Scott, she's from someplace called Fort MacLeod. She moved here this year. She says that every time she walks down the street people stop and stare because she's a new face. She's from away. So are you. People will know you're from away. They'll look. Let's go back to Bed and Roses and talk about this."

Leighla broke her silence. "There's nothing to talk about, Garrett. I want to have a little fun for once. I want to do something *I* want to do."

As we walked down Shore Road, I continued to search the yards, hoping I wouldn't see anybody. Good luck was on our side. Except for a couple of little kids playing in the park, the streets were deserted. When we reached Big Dock, I scanned the length of the dock. Luck was with us again.

No fishermen. Nobody was fixing nets or boats. Big Dock was minus people.

"Where's your boat, Garrett?" Leighla asked as we walked past the office of Glover's Marina.

At the same time, the office door opened, Mr. Glover stepped out, overheard the question and smiled at Leighla. "*The Estelle* is in slip thirty-one, my dear."

My guts floated in jelly. What would Mr. Glover do when he recognized Leighla? "Good evening, Garrett," Mr. Glover said. "I don't think I know this pretty young lady. She must be from away. Please introduce me."

Mr. G didn't know who she was. I hoped my sigh of relief didn't make him suspicious. On second thought, maybe it wasn't all that strange. Mr. Glover was a boat nut. He was always painting someone's boat in dry dock or grubbing around with someone's engine. I bet the only magazines he reads are about boats. He probably hardly ever watches TV.

Our good luck was continuing.

"Hi, Mr. G," I said. "This is Leighla. She's a guest at Bed and Roses for a few days."

Leighla and Mr. G exchanged hellos.

Mr. Glover stroked his bushy beard and grinned at Leighla. "I hope you enjoy your stay in Pirate Cove, young lady. And if you don't mind me saying so, you're very attractive. Perhaps you should consider becoming a . . . what's the word for people who pose in magazines and catalogs?"

"A model?" Leighla said.

"Yes, that's it," Mr. Glover said. "It's none of my business, of course, but I think you have looks to be a model, young lady."

Leighla made a secret wink in my direction. "Maybe I'll think about it, sir. I hear the job isn't everything it seems to be."

"Maybe not," Mr. G said as he locked the office door. "But like I said, you have that look." He waved a good-bye and sauntered away.

"Mr. Glover is an okay guy," I told Leighla.

"He looks so neat. I love his bushy beard." She noticed a row of buoys, spread out along the planks of the dock. "What are those big orange balloons for, Garrett?"

"They're not balloons. Those are lobster buoys. They're made out of hard plastic. Lobster fishermen tie them to their traps, so they'll be able to find them the next day. Those belong to my friend's father, Mr. Hayes. Orange with a blue dot. That's his marking."

"Lobster is one of my favorite foods. Do you like it?"

"I did until someone told me lobsters are scavengers. They eat dead fish and stuff on the bottom of the ocean. For some reason, that makes them seem less, umm . . . less tasty."

"I suppose," she said absently. "Where's slip number thirty-one? I want to see *The Estelle*."

I was about to point out that we should go back to Bed & Roses right away, how lucky she'd been that nobody had spotted her and luckier still that Mr. Glover didn't know who she was and how somebody could appear on Big Dock at any moment, but my pride in our boat got the better of me. I wanted to show off *The Estelle*. So I led Leighla to the wooden boat moored down the dock.

"She's an eighteen-foot Joycraft Bay Cruiser with a hundred and fifty horsepower inboard motor," I bragged. "My grandfather bought her when they were still making boats out of wood, rather than fiberglass. She's a classic piece of water transportation, solid mahogany and teak.

"It's beautiful," Leighla said.

"*The Estelle* is not an *it*," I explained. "She's a *she*. All boats and ships are female."

"I think I knew that. Can I sit in it? Can I sit in the driver's seat?"

A minute later, Leighla sat in the driver's seat of *The Estelle*. I sat in the passenger's seat, explaining the controls. "The black lever controls the gears. Push it forward, the boat goes that way. Push it back, the boat reverses. The red lever is the throttle, which is the same as a gas

58

pedal in a car. Forward, we go fast. Back, we stop."

"Can I drive it out?" she asked.

"Not a chance. Sorry. You need a license from the Pirate Cove Harbor Authority to take the wheel in the bay."

"Who are they?"

"They is he. Mr. Glover. He's the official Harbor Authority. He controls the licenses."

"Can't you ask him to let me drive?"

"No can do. There were a few serious accidents among the tourists a few years ago, so the town made a boat license a must-have. Mr. G takes his job seriously. You have to do a test."

"Figures," she grumbled. "Just when I was having the most fun I've had in a year."

I checked the fuel gauge. The white needle was almost touching the yellow *E,* the *empty* mark. "We couldn't go far, anyway. We're almost out of gas."

Leighla checked out the steering column and the dashboard. "Where's the key to start it?"

"You don't need one. Pump the throttle and press the red button in the middle of the wheel."

"No key? Does that mean anybody can start your boat?"

"I guess so."

"Aren't you afraid somebody might steal it?"

" 'Course not. This is Pirate Cove."

"That's incredible. In New York it seems that half the parked cars have those bars locked onto the steering wheels. Karl has a sign on the limo's dash that says NO RADIO IN CAR so people won't smash the windows. Jennifer used to have one on her own car too until somebody broke her window and wrote 'Get One' on the sign."

"Big city," I said. "I know what it's like. I used to live in Vancouver."

"Is that a gun?" She pointed at the flare pistol in the cubbyhole in the deck.

"It's a flare pistol. For emergencies."

"Is it loaded?"

"Not right now. I haven't got any flares."

A small insect, probably a sand fly, hovered in front of my face. I swatted at it and the bug fluttered into my right eye.

"Ow," I complained, rubbing my eye. "Something just flew into my eye."

"Don't do that. You're not supposed to rub it. You can make it worse. Let me have a look." Leighla pulled my hand away from my face and leaned close to me so she could check out my eye. "I see it," she said. "It's in the corner. Hold still. I'll wipe it out." She reached into her fanny pack, took out a clean Kleenex and twisted it into a cone shape. Then she raised her hand toward my face and with one gentle touch with the pointy end of the tissue, she removed the bug.

At the same time, there was a flash of light. Then another.

And another.

"Interesting," a voice said. "Most interesting."

I whipped my head in the direction of the dock, and saw a man dressed in a denim shirt and blue jeans, pointing an expensive-looking camera in our direction. There was another flash. Again and again. A lot more. Flash. Flash. Flash.

"Oh, no," Leighla said.

"Who are you?" I shouted at the photographer. "What is this?"

Leighla glared at him, a sour look on her face. "How did you know I was here, Dennis?"

"Dennis?" I exclaimed. "You know this guy, Leighla?"

She nodded. "Yeah, I know this creep. This is Dennis Fitzgerald. He gets in my face all the time. Remember Karl told you about him back at the inn. He sells his photos to the newspapers which pay the most money."

Dennis lowered his camera. "Hey, Leighla, come on. I'm not a creep. I may be a jerk, but I ain't a creep." He chuckled to himself. "And there's nothing wrong with making a buck. This is how our country got so great. And to answer your question, my lovely little Leighla, I found you 'cause like you said, I am your shadow."

"You're slime, Dennis," Leighla growled.

"Slime?" Dennis Fitzgerald said the word like he'd never heard it before. "Slime? I don't think so. I may be scum, but I ain't slime."

"How did you find me?" Leighla asked.

"I was parked outside your agency and saw the limo coming out of the underground parking. It was a no-brainer. I follow the limo, I get pictures of you. Hey, it was a long, long drive out here. A long, long, long drive. But it was worth it. What photos." Fitzgerald patted his camera. "I'm off to Disneyland with the bonus I get for these."

"Karl and Jennifer are going to be so mad," Leighla groaned.

"He can't do this," I said. "This isn't right. This is an invasion of your privacy." I jumped out of my seat, vaulted over the windshield, hopped, skipped and jumped off the bow of *The Estelle*, and charged at Fitzgerald. I grabbed the photographer's arm and tried to snatch the camera.

Fitzgerald lifted the Nikon above his head. "Hey, watch it, kid. You got the money to replace this, if you bust it?"

"You can't just take our picture without our permission!" I yelled.

He chuckled. "Don't they teach you about the constitution in school anymore? Geez, the education system in this country is going to pot."

Once more, I reached up to grab the camera and Dennis gave me a not-so-gentle push in the chest. "Hey, kid, you're starting to bug me." Then he turned and began to walk down Big Dock.

I wasn't about to give up. If I couldn't get what I wanted by force, I'd try being polite. "Please." I jogged beside Fitzgerald. "Don't do this, sir. It's not fair. It's not right."

"Fair? Right? Leighla Livingston is making a million bucks a year because she has a pretty face. You think that's right? Is that fair?"

"Leighla is in Pirate Cove because she had to get away," I pleaded. "Get away from people like you. Give her a break."

That made him laugh. "Listen, kid. When you decide you want to be famous, you adopt a truckload of people like me at the same time." He looked up at the sky. "Gosh, I wish I was a kid again. I wish I didn't know now what I didn't know then."

"I'll pay you for those pictures," I offered.

We got to the end of Big Dock, reached the parking lot and a beat-up Ford Tempo. "You'll pay me? Cool."

"I've got two hundred dollars in my savings account. Almost."

"Almost two hundred? That's touching, but it ain't enough by a couple of decimal points."

"Think about Leighla, sir," I continued to appeal for Leighla. "She needs a vacation. If you tell the papers she's here, you'll ruin everything."

He opened the car door. "Hey, little buddy, you should be thanking me. When these photos appear in the newspapers, you'll become an overnight celebrity. You might even be a feature on *Entertainment Tonight*. I'm giving you your fifteen minutes of fame."

One last try. "If you give me your film, I'll give you my '61 Roger Maris baseball card."

He stopped. "You got a '61 Maris, kid? A Topp's '61?"

"My father collected it when he was young. He gave it to me."

"Wow. Number two in the set. I'm a big ball fan. I got the 1961 Topp's set except for six cards. Roger Maris is one of the cards I need."

"It's in mint shape, Mr. Fitzgerald."

"Mint? Interesting. There ain't many mint left. And you'd give it to me for these photos?"

I nodded.

"Well, believe it or not, I'm sort of moved."

"I'll run home and get the card."

He scratched his armpit as he thought. "Naw, don't bother. When I sell these photos I'll be able to buy a half dozen complete '61 sets. But I'll tell you what. Because I'm not a creep, and because you were going to give me your Maris, I'll do you a favor. I won't tell the paper where Leighla is. I'll let her have a couple of days without guys like me bugging you." He glanced at the sky. "I'm getting soft in my old age." Fitzgerald hopped into his car. Fifteen seconds later he was out of sight.

Leighla walked up beside me.

"I'm sorry," I told her. "I couldn't get the pictures."

"I'm going to get in mega-trouble," she said.

"I was worried about you!" Karl's angry voice called from the boardwalk. "Why are you here?"

"Karl, I . . ." Leighla's voice trailed off.

A softer but equally angry voice called, "Garrett Hawgood, what are you doing?"

I focused on two figures at the end of the dock, Karl's hands rested on his hips. His face was carved into an if-looks-could-kill mask. Gram's arms were folded across her chest.

"Come here, Miss Livingston!" Karl ordered.

"Go to your room, Garrett!" Gram directed.

"Go to my room? We're on Big Dock."

"You are both in serious trouble," Karl proclaimed. "Serious trouble."

It was ten o'clock when Hornbeck brought me a tray of cookies and a mug of hot milk. "Gram wants you to have these," he told me. "I'm going to bed now."

"Is Gram still angry?" I asked.

"Not as much," he answered.

"I can't believe she sent me to my room. I'm in

65

eighth grade. What kind of punishment is this? Sent to my room?"

"Karl and the witch lady were real mad, too," Hornbeck said. "They shouted at Leighla so loud, they made her cry."

"I could hear them from up here. Maybe Leighla was wrong leaving the house without telling them, but they should understand. They should know how stressed she is."

Hornbeck yawned. "You think she could have been kidnapped, like the witch lady said?"

"The witch lady has a name. It's polite to call her Jennifer. And I don't think anybody in Pirate Cove would kidnap her. Except maybe Butcher."

"Is it true your picture is going to be in the papers? You and the pretty girl?"

"It looks that way."

"What will Stacey say when she sees you?"

"I don't know. Listen, thanks for the cookies, Bro. You look pretty tired. Maybe you should go to bed."

"You want to hear what happened to Baker?"

I munched on a cookie and nodded my head. "Sure."

"Butcher dyed him tonight."

I nearly choked on chocolate chips. What did Hornbeck mean? Surely . . . no! "Butcher murdered his brother?" I gasped.

## chapter 6

Hornbeck scrunched his face. "No. Butcher didn't kill Baker. Why do you think that?"

"Because you said he 'died' him."

"That's right. Butcher dyed Baker all purple. Baker says he's not going to school until it wears off."

"Oh, he *d-y-e-d* him," I said with relief. "I thought you meant . . . wait a minute. How did Butcher dye Baker?"

"Baker called me an hour ago and told me all about it. Baker takes a shower every night. He said today Butcher took off the thing on the shower."

"The thing?"

"Where the water comes out."

"The shower head?"

"That's it. Baker said Butcher filled the shower head thing with grape Kool-Aid and put it back on. When Baker turned on the water it sprayed him purple. He says it won't wash off. He tried, but it's still there."

Despite the downer the evening had become, I couldn't stop a smile. "So that's how Butcher planned to rack Baker. I've got to give it to the big guy. He's a genius in his own way. Kool-Aid in the shower head. Brilliant."

"Can I ask you a question, Garrett?"

I took a sip of milk. "Go for it."

"Travis told me about boys and girls and stuff. Is it true?"

"Boys and girls? Stuff?" I had a feeling what the "stuff" was, but I asked anyway. "What did Travis tell you?"

"It's kind of scary."

"Tell me anyway."

Hornbeck leaned over and whispered into my ear.

"Travis told you that?"

Hornbeck nodded. "Is that true?"

Stacey was right, Travis really did need to talk to somebody. Half of what he told Hornbeck was mixed-up. "No, it's not true, Hornbeck."

My little brother blew a sigh of relief.

"Listen, Bro, I promised Stacey I'd talk to Travis about stuff like that. Why don't you bring him home after school tomorrow? The three of us can have a little talk."

"Okay, Garrett. What do you think I should be for Halloween?"

"I could make you into a pretty decent vampire."

"I want to be something different. Like Travis."

"Travis dressing up as a girl is not all that original."

"I guess not. Travis said I should go out as a used Kleenex."

"A what?"

"Either that or a toilet plunger. Travis said I'd be perfect for both of them because they suit my demeanor."

"And Travis is your friend?"

"What's a demeanor?"

"I'll tell you later."

"Okay. Good night, Garrett."

After I changed into my *Sesame Street* pajamas—another part of the joke birthday gift from my folks—I lay in bed, completely awake, a million light years from sleep. I could hear Karl's muffled snores from Second Floor Back, the room beneath me. What a mess. There was a good chance my picture would be in tomorrow's newspapers. Me and Leighla Livingston. What was I going to tell Stacey?

There was a weak knock on the door. "Garrett," Leighla said softly from the other side. "Can I come in?"

"Sure."

I rolled over and flicked on the light.

"Can I talk to you?" Leighla eased silently into the room, closed the door, and sat on the end of my bed. She was dressed in a rumpled white robe. Her hair was tied into a crooked ponytail and her eyelids were red and puffy. Even disheveled, she looked great.

"Are you okay?" I asked. "I can tell you've been crying."

"I must look like a complete mess."

"Actually, you don't."

Her face broke into a feeble smile. "Thanks. You're really sweet."

"That's what all famous supermodels tell me."

The smile creases deepened a little. "I came to thank you for standing up for me this afternoon. For going after the photographer."

"It was nothing."

"Yes, it was. Thank you."

"You're welcome."

"Garrett, I've decided to quit. I don't want to be me anymore. I want to go back home to St. Albert. I want to live with my mom and dad and sister. I don't want to put up with people like Dennis Fitzgerald. I don't want to put up with

Karl and Jennifer running my life, shouting at me."

I thought about it. "You don't want to be rich and famous and be on TV?"

She shook her head. "Not anymore."

"Gee, Leighla, I don't know. Maybe you should think about it some more. To me, rich and famous sound like good things to be."

"They're such wonderful things that when I go on vacation, I have to hide out. People chase me, trying to take my photo. I need a bodyguard and a manager to run my life. I have no friends. You're the first boy I've talked to in months."

"I agree, your life could be a *little* better. But aren't those hassles worth it to be famous?"

"I'm not famous because I've done something special. I'm famous because I can smile and take a good picture."

"It's a great smile."

"You don't understand. Nobody understands." She started crying.

"Umm, Leighla?" I didn't know what to do. "Stop crying, okay? Everything is going to be all right."

She cried harder.

By instinct, I did what I do when Hornbeck is upset. I reached forward and hugged her.

"I'm going to call Mom first thing tomorrow

71

morning," she said between sobs. "She'll understand. She'll *have* to understand."

I'm not sure how long it took for Leighla's weeping to slow to a whimper—three minutes, probably more. I didn't say anything the whole time. I simply held her tight. At one point, I caught myself humming something which might have been a lullaby I'd heard when I was a little kid. Who knows?

When Leighla was all cried out, she whispered, "Can I sleep in your room tonight? I don't want to be alone."

I released my hug hold and stood up, suddenly embarrassed my pj's were covered with images of Burt and Ernie and Cookie Monster, suddenly embarrassed I'd been hugging the world's most famous young supermodel. "I'm not sure that would be, ah . . . right, Leighla. If you don't want to be alone, maybe you should go to Jennifer's room."

"I guess Jennifer would understand. You're probably right," she murmured, as she stretched across the bed, then slowly coiled into a fetal position. "You're prob . . ." Her voice diminished into shallow breathing.

"Leighla," I said. "Are you still awake? Leighla? Leighla? Wake up, Leighla."

She was in another dimension.

I sighed, thought about going downstairs to tell

Jennifer or Gram, then decided against it because I had the feeling it would get both of us into deeper trouble. Besides, Leighla looked so peaceful, scrunched up like a baby, it was probably best to let her sleep.

And what do they say? Vision in hindsight is twenty-twenty. If I'd gone downstairs at that moment, then . . . well, then the next day wouldn't have happened.

But once more I didn't tell. Instead I grabbed a blanket from the linen closet and a pillow off the bed, squeezed myself into the armchair, got as comfortable as possible, and, with the sound of Leighla's breathing and Karl's distant, dull snoring, thought about what Leighla had just said.

"She's making a mistake," I said to myself. Sure, being famous had a few minor drawbacks. But in the end, wasn't fame a good thing to have? Throw in a few million bucks and, hey, what was the problem? If it were me, *I* wouldn't quit. Then it hit me like I'd been struck by lightning.

I thought about playing hockey in Vancouver and started to realize that maybe I understood what Leighla was talking about after all. When I finally felt the first wave of drowsiness, I picked up my igloo fantasy.

\*      \*      \*

Stacey and I are trapped in an igloo, imprisoned by a raging Arctic blizzard.

"Oh, Garrett," Stacey says in my imagination. "I'm so frightened."

"There's no problem," I assure her. "The blizzard will be over in a week or two."

"Whatever are we going to do for all that time?" Stacey wonders.

"We'll think of something," I answer.

"It's so cold in here." Stacey shivers.

"Then I guess the first thing we should do is cuddle to stay warm. You know, hug and stuff."

"No way," she says. "You had your picture taken with Leighla Livingston. And I thought you were my boyfriend."

Poof!

When I awoke the next morning, Leighla was gone. I stretched the stiffness out of my arms and glanced at the clock. Eight o'clock. "Geez," I muttered. "It's late."

I must have forgotten to set the alarm, something I do at least once a week. But if I sleep in, Gram usually wakes me at seven-thirty. Where was she this morning? Gram gets up at dawn.

On the way to the bathroom I noticed Third Floor Front, Leighla's room, was empty. I skipped my morning shower to save time and dressed quickly. On my way downstairs, I saw the two guest rooms on the second floor were vacant, too. I was surprised to find only Hornbeck in the kitchen. He was leaning forward, holding his ear over a bowl of Rice Krispies.

"Morning, Bro. What are you doing?"

"I'm trying to hear the 'snap, crackle, pop.' Travis says you can hear them go 'snap, crackle, pop' when you pour on milk."

"Can you?"

"It's true. They sound like they're on fire."

I grabbed a bowl and helped myself to some cereal. "I slept in. How come Gram didn't wake me?"

"She's not here."

"Gram's not here? She should be cooking breakfast for the guests. Where is everybody?"

"Don't know."

"Strange."

"I heard Gram talking to Karl and the witch lady real early," Hornbeck said. "They sounded upset."

"Upset? You mean *angry* upset?"

"Maybe. Karl was saying bad words like he was mad. But the witch lady was crying."

"I wonder . . ."

Our kitchen door burst open and Butcher blasted in, the *Portland Times* newspaper in his hand. "All right, Hawgood! You cool dude." He tossed the newspaper on the kitchen table. It was folded to the entertainment section. There, filling

75

a quarter page, was a full color picture of Leighla Livingston and me, sitting in the front seat of *The Estelle.*

I've never, ever fainted in my whole life, but I came real close to passing out at that moment. Leighla had her hand near my face, about to wipe the bug out of the corner of my eye. But because of the angle, you couldn't see the Kleenex in her hand and it looked as if she was touching my cheek. Leighla was leaning close, peering into my eye. It looked as if we were on the verge of a kiss.

Butcher thumped my back, causing an eruption of Rice Krispies from my mouth. They exploded over the tablecloth and into my brother's face.

"Gross," Hornbeck whined.

As I wiped up the milk and half-eaten cereal with a napkin, I read the blurb under the photo:

> *So this is how a supermodel spends her vacation? A photographer caught world-famous young teen model, Leighla Livingston, and an unidentified young man enjoying each other's company. Miss Livingston is on vacation somewhere in Maine.*

At least Dennis kept his promise to keep Pirate Cove a secret. Leighla was wrong. He was just a jerk, not a creep.

Hornbeck cleaned his face with the sleeve of his sweat shirt and checked out the paper. "You didn't tell me you were kissy-facing with Leighla, Garrett."

"I'm not kissing her," I defended. "It just looks that way."

"Huh?" Butcher wondered. "What does this have to do with cooks in May?"

Obviously Butcher's hearing wasn't any better. "I'm not kissing her. She's getting a bug out of my eye."

Butcher erupted into his deep belly laugh. "She's getting a bug out of your eye. Right. And I'm a ballet dancer. Tell me another, Hawgood."

"It really looks like you're kissy-facing," Hornbeck said as he stood up and put his bowl in the dishwasher. "I'm going to go see Baker to find out if he's going to school. I want to see if he's still all purple."

"What, Hornbeck?" Butcher asked. "You're going to the pool to see if Baker is a tall turtle?"

Hornbeck giggled and left Bed & Roses through the back door.

"Weird little kid," Butcher said as he sat beside me. He thumped the photo with his finger. "I was eating breakfast with my old man. He was reading the paper and he asked me 'Isn't that Garrett Hawgood? Isn't that his boat?' So I look and I figure there's no way it could be you kissing

Leighla Livingston. I mean, she wouldn't kiss a nerd like you, right? Then I checked out the boat and I see *The Estelle* on the bow and I nearly dropped a brick."

I raised my voice so Butcher could hear me. "Nerd?"

"Don't take it personal, Hawgood. I like you anyway. And not only do I like you, now I respect you. I mean that. You must have something special to get a kiss from her."

"I hope Stacey doesn't see this."

"She already has. I called her and told her."

"You called her? Why?"

"Because she's my cousin. I thought she was your girlfriend. You don't kiss other girls if you've got a girlfriend."

"We're not kissing," I insisted for the third time. "It just looks that way."

Butcher patted my back again. "It sure does. Kissing Leighla Livingston. Awesome! Leighla has got to be staying here, huh? That's who was in that limo I saw on Old Mill Road, right? That's who was wearing the Minx perfume, wasn't it? I should be snarling at you for lying to me, but I understand why. I wouldn't tell you if Leighla Livingston was in my house. Where is she?"

"I don't know."

"Her stuff is in one of your guests rooms, huh? Do you mind if I go upstairs and look at it?"

I stared at him. "Get serious."

The front doorbell rang.

"Excuse me," I said.

"No problem," Butcher replied. "Is it okay if I help myself to a bowl of cereal?"

"I thought you said you ate breakfast?"

"Just a little one. A couple of eggs and some sausages. That was a half-hour ago."

"Help yourself," I told him as I walked into the hallway. When I saw the silhouette of the bell-ringer through the lace curtain on the front door window, the little food I'd eaten formed a miniature cannonball in my stomach. For a moment, I thought about tiptoeing up to my room, locking the door and hiding out for the rest of my life. But I knew that would only postpone the inevitable. I was going to have to face Stacey Bowman sometime.

I opened the door. "Hello, Stacey," I said. "It's not what you think it is."

She gazed back at me, her eyes focused on mine.

"Leighla's a guest and I was taking her out to Hole's Island," I nervously explained. "She was taking a bug out of my eye. I know the photo looks like . . . it wasn't like that. Honest."

Stacey's green pupils remained transfixed on

79

my eyes. Then, ever so slowly, her eyelids fluttered, ever so slightly. A tear appeared in her right eye and lazily flowed down her chin. Then an identical tear cascaded down her left cheek.

"Stacey," I said. "It's not what it looks like."

She turned and walked away.

"Stacey!" I called. "Stacey!"

She didn't turn around.

I watched her walk down Shore Road until she turned the corner and I couldn't see her anymore. "Just great," I said out loud to no one. "Just absolutely great."

I looked up and noticed how the weather matched my mood. The sky was blocked by low, dark clouds. The air had turned from Indian summer into late fall, overnight. A few miles offshore, a dark wall was drifting across the north Atlantic toward land. A fog bank. In a short time Pirate Cove was going to be covered in a thick, dreary mist. And, because I felt so rotten, I welcomed the thought.

When I went back to the kitchen, Butcher was gone. Which was okay because I didn't feel like talking to him, or rather, shouting to him anymore. There were five banana peels on the kitchen table, the entire contents of the fruit bowl. The Rice Krispies box was empty.

I was pouring the rest of my half-eaten bowl of cereal into the garborator when Gram burst through the door. Her face was flushed and she was a little out of breath. She wore an expression I'd never seen before. Fear.

"Oh, Garrett," she said. "Something terrible has happened."

chapter 7

I knew without asking the "something terrible" had to do with Leighla.

"I came back to get you, Garrett," Gram said. "I want you to go to Lookoff Point. See if Leighla's gone there."

My hunch was right. "Lookoff Point? Why would Leighla go to Lookoff Point this early in the morning? What's going on?"

Gram got a glass from the cupboard and filled it with water from the faucet. She took a short drink. She fanned her face with her hand and blew out a breath. "I can't think of where else she would be. She's missing, Garrett. I'm so worried."

"Missing? How?"

"Leighla came down to use the phone just after dawn," Gram explained. "I heard her and got out of bed to see if everything was all right. She was talking to her mother."

"How do you know that?"

"Because she kept on repeating, 'Please, Mom' over and over. I'm not sure what they were talking about, but I could tell her mother wasn't happy. I could hear her mother shouting over the phone from six feet away. Leighla hung up and ran to her room, crying. That's the last time we saw her. Sometime between six and seven o'clock, she must have sneaked out of Bed and Roses."

"When did you find out Leighla was gone?"

"When Jennifer came down at seven. Jennifer said she'd found a note on Leighla's bed in Third Floor Front."

"What did the note say?"

" 'Nobody understands.' That's all. 'Nobody understands.' Then Karl came down and got very angry. Jennifer became upset. So we went outside to look for Leighla."

"How come you didn't wake me?"

Gram took another drink of water. "It was all happening so fast. I didn't think. We've contacted Sheriff Carson. I'm so concerned, Garrett."

"I'm sure everything is all right. This is Pirate Cove."

"If that nasty photographer found her, other strange people could have, too. Jennifer told me Leighla gets disturbing phone calls." Gram tapped her temple. "From people who are not all there."

"We'd better find her," I agreed. "But I doubt she's gone to Lookoff Point. Leighla doesn't even know where that is."

"Take your bike and check out there anyway," Gram insisted. "Where else could she be? I'm going to go down the street and ask the neighbors if they've seen anything." Gram left her glass of water on the sink and exited through the back door.

Remembering how cool it was, I ran into the hallway to get my denim jacket. Where are you, Leighla? I thought. Why'd you run away? For a moment, I wondered if I should have been more sympathetic when Leighla came into my room last night. Could I have said or done something to help her?

Then I froze.

I knew she was there even before I twisted around. It was the same feeling I'd had in my dream yesterday afternoon. I *sensed* her presence. When I turned, the girl from my dream stood on the landing at the top of the stairs.

She was only there for a fraction of a fraction of a second. But her image was burned into my memory.

In my dream, I thought she was wearing a white, baggy-sleeved blouse. When I saw her on the stairs I could see it was the top of an old-fashioned white dress. And she was wearing black leggings or socks with ankle-high granny boots. The girl peered down at me through her long black bangs.

Suddenly my skin got a size too tight.

"I saw her," I whispered. "The girl was there. Real. Standing at the top of the stairs, watching me. . . ."

I swallowed away my dry throat.

"Don't be stupid," a voice in my head said. "Look. There's nothing there. It was just your imagination."

"No," I said out loud. "I definitely saw something there."

I wiped the thin layer of sweat off my forehead and glanced out the window.

And I quickly pushed the girl out of my thoughts. Because I knew exactly where Leighla had gone.

I threw open the front door and gazed across the half mile of water at Hole's Island. From this distance, I couldn't see anything. I took off for Big Dock.

Three minutes later, I stood in front of empty slip thirty-one of Big Dock. *The Estelle* wasn't there anymore. Which meant I was right. Leighla had gone to Hole's Island.

Mr. Glover walked out of the marina office and

down Big Dock. "Where's *The Estelle,* Garrett?" he called.

I pointed at the island. "Hole's Island. Leighla, the girl I was with yesterday, she took her out."

"She's not allowed to do that," Mr. G noted. "You need a license to . . ."

I spun around. "I know that," I interrupted. "Leighla is . . . she's a little mixed-up right now. Will you do me a favor, Mr. G? Would you give me a ride out to Hole's Island so I can get her and the boat?"

He rubbed his bushy whiskers. "I think there's a bit of a story behind this."

"Please don't say or do anything, Mr. Glover. I promise Leighla won't drive the boat anymore."

Mr. G continued to stroke his beard. "Well, it's not my usual way, but maybe this one time."

"So you'll take me over?"

"Yes, I will. Providing you do a favor in return. I have to go to Bay of Bays on Saturday to pick up some lobster traps. I could use a little help."

"You've got it," I replied.

He tipped his hat. "Then let's go to the Captain's Island."

The only place on Hole's Island to land a boat is the old stone dock. Once upon a time, it was covered with a wooden boardwalk. The only things left of the boardwalk are a few support posts thrusting through the boulders like petri-fied tree trunks. As Mr. G's boat rounded the tip of the island, I saw *The Estelle* tied to one of those posts.

Mr. Glover idled his boat beside the rocks so I could jump ashore. "Don't be too long out there," he warned.

I checked the water level on the rocks. "It's still three hours until low tide. I won't be that long."

"I'm not talking about low tide, Garrett." He pointed out to the ocean. "The fog bank will reach us pretty soon."

"No problem," I told him. "I've been out here in fog before. I know how to follow the horn."

"That may be. But never take fog too lightly. Always be afraid of fog, Garrett," Mr. Glover warned. "Always be afraid. Take care, boy."

"Thanks, Mr. G."

"I trust this won't be repeated," he said. Then he roared back towards Big Dock and I started jogging over the uneven ground and through shrub pines to reach the old mansion. It was the only place Leighla could be.

Because there are no boards on the windows of the old house, the rain, snow and frost have eroded most of the inside walls down to the mar-ble. Most of the upper bedrooms have been sealed shut because the flooring has disintegrated to the point where it's dangerous to walk on.

But the thick, oak hardwood flooring of the main hallway and staircases is still in pretty good shape. I found Leighla sitting on the bottom step of the old stairway, without a jacket, shivering, her arms wrapped around her knees, her face soiled by tear streaks.

Leighla looked up and watched me approach when she heard my footsteps. For the longest time, neither of us said anything. I wanted to shout at her. I wanted to scream, "What the heck are you doing out here? Don't you know how stupid you are? What if you'd driven the boat onto the rocks? How come you don't have a jacket? It's forty-five degrees!" But I didn't. I just stood in front of her and forced a smile.

Finally, Leighla said a simple, "Hello, Garrett." The cool, damp air steamed her breath. "How did you get here?"

"Mr. Glover gave me a ride. You've got everyone so scared," I removed my jacket and draped it around her shoulders. "What are you doing here, Leighla?"

"I had to be by myself. I figured it would take Karl a while to find me here. How did you know I'd come to the mansion?"

"I had a hunch."

"I called my mom this morning," she said. "I told her I didn't want to do what I'm doing anymore. I told her I didn't want to live in New York

88

with Jennifer, that I wanted to come home and live with my family. Do you know what she did?"

"Gram told me. Your mom got mad."

"She called me ungrateful. She said millions of girls would die to be me and I should appreciate how lucky I am. *Lucky*? The last thing I am is lucky." She waved a hand in the air. "My life is like this old house. Outside, it looks neat. Inside, it's a hollow, rotten mess. Mom doesn't understand. The agency doesn't understand. Jennifer and Karl don't understand. Nobody understands. You don't understand."

"I didn't last night," I said. "Now I think I do. I want to talk to you, Leighla. But I want to talk to you someplace warm."

I held out my hand to help her stand up. She did. "Okay, Garrett, I don't know what I'm doing here either. Let's go back to Bed and Roses."

We threaded our way across the rocks and through the shrub pines back to the boat. At one point, Leighla asked, "Who used to live in the mansion, Garrett?"

"Nobody. There's a real sad story behind the place. It was built by an old New England sea captain, Frederick Hole, for a woman he'd met in Scotland. He was going to bring her to Maine, get married and raise a family, but she died before coming to the States. The captain was so destroyed, he just left the place."

"How awful," Leighla said.

"Did you see the small house by the dock? The one that's all boarded up?"

"Yes, was that built for the servants?" Leighla asked.

"Nope. It was going to be the playhouse for the captain's kids. Kids that were never born. There's a tunnel connecting the two places. There was going to be a miniature railroad for the kids to ride to their playhouse."

"Some people have such unlucky lives, don't they?"

"Gram always says, 'There, by the grace of God, go I.' It means bad stuff can happen at any moment. When you least expect it."

Leighla got quiet. Maybe she was thinking about her life.

When we got to *The Estelle,* I said, "You know, Leighla, for somebody who hasn't driven a boat before, you sure did a good job docking it. It's not an easy thing to do."

"I know," she said. "I had to try it four times before I got close enough to throw the rope over the post."

I hopped into the driver's seat and pressed the starter button. Leighla pulled the rope off the old pylon and climbed into the passenger seat. I pressed the red throttle lever forward and steered the boat into deeper water, so we'd turn the point and cruise the half mile back to Big Dock. And I couldn't wait to get home. I felt more than cold.

"What's that?" Leighla pointed at the dark wall of the fog bank. "I saw that when I came out here, but it was further away. It's a lot closer now. Is it fog?"

"That's right," I told her. "Sometimes it comes in like that. Like a dark wall. It's kind of spooky when it hits you. One second everything is clear and the next you have trouble seeing your shoes."

"It looks like the cover of a horror book."

"A lot of old people in Pirate Cove believe ghost ships sail in the fog. My grandmother does."

"Ghost ships?"

"Gram thinks shipwrecks rise from the bottom of the ocean in the fog. Kind of dumb, huh?"

Leighla actually shivered.

"Gram says the dead crews sail the seas looking for . . ." I stopped.

"Looking for what?"

"I'm not freaking you out, am I?" I asked.

She nodded. "Yes, you are. But I don't want you to stop. Looking for what?"

"Looking for people lost in the fog. If you're lost and a ghost ship finds you, the dead sailors snatch you away. When the fog lifts, the ghost ship returns to the bottom of the sea. And you go down with it. The living join the dead."

"What a gruesome story." Leighla shivered.

"You ever heard of the *Mary Celeste*?"

Leighla shook her head.

"It was a ship found bobbing in the Atlantic, completely abandoned. Its cargo was still there. There were no signs of any kind of violence. The table was set for breakfast. It was like the crew just jumped overboard. Gram says the *Mary Celeste* met a ghost ship."

"That's a true story?"

"There are dozens of stories like that. Believe it or not, Pirate Cove oldtimers sing "Amazing Grace" if they get caught out in a fog. They believe the hymn makes the dead sailors cry."

Leighla looked puzzled. "It does? Why?"

"Because "Amazing Grace" is the hymn that's played at most funerals. It's supposed to remind the ghosts of their families and friends they left behind. The ghosts start to cry and they forget about you."

"I'll never think about fog the same way."

"Gram also says . . ."

Suddenly, *The Estelle*'s motor coughed twice, sputtered a few times and died.

"What's wrong?" Leighla asked. "Why did we stop?"

"I don't know." I pressed the ignition button.

All I heard was the whirr of the starter motor. Mr. Glover had just tuned the engine a couple of weeks ago. It had never stalled before.

Then I noticed the fuel gauge. The white needle rested directly on the yellow *E*. In frustration I thumped the side of my head with the palm of my hand. "We're out of gas. I should have remembered. I saw it last night. I should have brought a can of gas with me." I punched the steering wheel. "How could I be so stupid?"

"I'm sorry," Leighla apologized. "This is all my fault."

I wanted to turn to her and say, "Yes, it is. If you hadn't been such a dipstick." I didn't. Instead I punched the steering wheel a second time.

"Do you have some paddles? We can paddle," she suggested.

"There are no paddles!" I snapped. "You can't paddle an eighteen-foot Joycraft! Don't you know *anything* about boats?"

Leighla grimaced at my anger.

Instinctively, I reached into the cubbyhole for the flare gun, then left it there. I remembered there were no flares either. What was it those old Laurel and Hardy guys said in their films? "This is a fine mess you've gotten us into." That's what I felt like shouting into Leighla's face. Again, I didn't. Instead, I said, "I'm sorry I got mad, Leighla. Getting mad isn't going to help us."

"It's all right, Garrett. I understand. I'd be more than mad if I were you."

"There's got to be something we can do. Let me think."

"Do you have a radio?" Leighla wanted to know.

I shook my head.

I watched Hole's Island. We were slowly drifting away from it, drifting into deeper water, drifting out to sea.

Leighla glanced into the back of *The Estelle*. "What's that big can back there?"

Leighla had spotted the anchor, a five gallon paint can full of cement. "The anchor," I told her.

"Can the anchor stop us from drifting?" she wondered.

"If we were in the bay it could. Out here the water is too deep. Hole's Island marks the edge of the shelf. The ocean floor drops a straight half mile. Our anchor rope is only long enough for the bottom of the bay."

"Maybe we'll drift back to the island or into shore," Leighla said hopefully.

There was no chance of that. Hole's Island was getting smaller second by second. "Low tide is coming," I told her. "The current is pulling us out to sea." I searched the horizon in every direction, hoping to spot a fishing boat. Nothing. We were alone.

"Are we in trouble, Garrett?"

"Not really," I lied.

"You're lying, Garrett. I can tell. I can tell by your voice. You're lying. Tell me the truth. We're in trouble, aren't we?"

"Yeah," I said. "We're in trouble, Leighla. In fact, we're in big trouble."

chapter 8

Leighla shifted in the passenger seat. "Why are we in such big trouble?" she demanded. "Tell me the truth, Garrett."

I pointed toward the east. "Because of that."

Leighla looked in the direction of my finger. The wall of fog was fifty yards away. It's face seemed to reach from water to sky. It moved across the gentle Atlantic swells like a creature on a hunt, a predator moving toward its prey. The misty front oozed and undulated as if it were alive and breathing. Behind the wall was darkness. I shivered, but it wasn't because I was cold.

The fog covered those fifty yards in fifty seconds. Neither Leighla or I said anything. It reached the front of *The Estelle,* the windshield, then us. As it passed us, I heard a little cry. I'm not sure which one of us made it. Maybe we both did.

The temperature immediately dropped another five degrees. The world turned from morning to dusk in an instant. The sound of the waves lapping the sides of *The Estelle* became muted and dull. The air hung heavy with a sour dankness. I couldn't see the stern of the boat. Leighla turned hazy.

She stated the obvious. "Now, nobody will be able to see us." Her voice was deadened by the dampness. "Garrett, what are we going to do?"

I didn't answer. I had no idea what we were going to do. None at all. At first, I thought about downplaying the mess we were in. Tell Leighla "Sure, we're in big trouble but things will turn out okay." But I knew I couldn't. Leighla had the right to know how bad things were, how much real trouble we were in. "You're right, Leighla. *Nobody* will be able to find us in this fog. And the low tide current is pulling us away from the shore. We're being sucked into deeper water."

"That's not good news, is it?"

"It's definitely bad news. We're in a boat made to cruise in shallow water, where it's calm. The further from shore, the rougher it gets. The north Atlantic gets real choppy this time of year. *The Estelle* wasn't built for major swells. and then there's . . ." I let my voice trail off.

97

"There's what?"

"The cold."

It was forty degrees and I was dressed in a T-shirt. What was the word Miss Scott had used when she was talking about how cold it was where she came from? For people who weren't dressed right and got caught outside when the weather tuned cold?

Hypothermia, a voice in my head said. It's called hypothermia. Remember? Miss Scott says it happens when you lose too much body heat too fast. Like you are right now. You're shivering. That's the first stage of hypothermia. You don't have to worry about *The Estelle* in rough water, Garrett, old boy. There's a good chance you'll be dead before that happens.

"The cold," I repeated. "That's our biggest problem. It's almost freezing and we have one jean jacket between us."

Leighla noticed my distress. "I'm sorry. I wasn't thinking. You're so cold." She removed my jacket from her shoulders. "Here."

"No, I'm all right."

"Don't be stupid, Garrett. You're shaking," she reasoned. "We'll share the jacket. You wear it for a couple of minutes. Then I'll wear it."

I was too cold to argue. So I nodded and slipped the jacket on. Leighla crossed her arms and shrunk her body as tight as possible to stay warm.

For a minute, maybe two or three, we didn't say anything. We just stared into the creamy grayness searching for . . . what? There was no way we'd be able to see anything. Heck, an aircraft carrier could pass by ten yards away and we wouldn't know it was there. It was like we'd been suddenly plunged into the middle of a marshmallow. We were surrounded by sticky, thick mist.

"Garrett," Leighla said. "The tide will change, won't it? Won't the tide eventually push us back into shore?"

"It would if we could stay right here," I explained. "But it's still another couple of hours before high tide. By then we'll have drifted into the deep currents. They'll take us north."

"Canada is up there," she said. "Will they push us to Canada?"

"No. I've been out fishing with Delton's dad. When he reaches the deep currents, like the Gulf Stream, he turns off his engine, drops his nets and lets the boat drift. He told me that he could drift all the way to Europe if he wanted."

Leighla's face suddenly brightened. "There's fishing boats out in the ocean?"

"A lot of them."

"Then when the fog lifts, a fishing boat could find us?"

"I hope so, Leighla. But I'm not sure when the fog will burn off. This fog is so thick. Sometimes fogs like this last for days."

"Maybe this isn't one of those fogs," Leighla suggested hopefully. "Maybe it'll only last a short time."

"It's possible." I tried to sound enthusiastic.

Not a chance, I thought. This is pea soup quality fog.

"If there was only some way we could stop from drifting," I said. "If there was only some way to stop and wait for high tide."

"I'm scared, Garrett. I've never . . . nothing like this has ever happened to me before."

"Leighla, I . . . I'm scared too."

We heard a dull distant moaning sound in the fog. It was followed by a lower, longer moan.

"What's that?" Leighla asked. "What are those noises?"

"Foghorns," I told her. "When you can't see the lighthouse on Hole's Island, they sound the horns."

The moans repeated themselves.

"The first one is a warning horn," I explained. "It's on the island. It lets you know you're getting too close. The longer one is on Big Dock. It guides you home. Gram once told me the sounds remind her of a cow and a calf calling each another."

Leighla shuffled her feet, trying to get a little more comfortable. Her bottom lip was shaking. I took off the jacket and handed it to her.

"No," she said. "You've only had it a few minutes."

"It's your turn."

She quickly slipped the jacket on.

Again, we spent a few minutes in the gray, dreary fog, not speaking. The only sounds were the fog horns and the swells softly slapping the sides of *The Estelle*. Except for that, there was incredible silence. It was so quiet I heard the tha-dump of my heart inside my ears.

And I got colder. My teeth began chattering.

"Are we going to die out here, Garrett?" Leighla asked flatly.

"Die? Of course not. Don't be silly."

"I'm not stupid," she said. "I heard everything you've been saying. There's almost no chance of someone finding us. We're drifting into rough water in a boat that wasn't built for it. Even if we don't sink, we could freeze." She pointed overboard. "You can't drink ocean water. And I know if you don't have any water, you're in trouble in less than a day."

"It's going to be okay, Leighla." I'm sure she knew I didn't believe it.

She took off my jacket and was about to hand it to me. "Here. your turn." She suddenly stopped.

"Wait. I have an idea, Garrett. Let's wear it together. That way we'll keep each other warm. I read a story once about a boy and a dog who got lost in the wilderness. Even though the temperature was below zero, the boy stayed alive because he kept hugging the dog. The dog's warmth kept him alive."

I was so cold sharing the jacket sounded like a wonderful idea.

I shoved my left arm into the left sleeve of the jacket, shifted closer to Leighla and threw the jacket around her shoulders. She struggled to get her right arm into the other sleeve so we were sharing the denim. We mashed against each other so tightly, it was almost uncomfortable. Our faces were less than a foot apart. But I began to warm up.

I smiled at her and she smiled back. "Hey, we must look completely stupid," I said. "But your idea is going to keep us warm. Smart thinking."

"I'm sorry I was so stupid to take *The Estelle* to the island," Leighla said. "Was Karl really angry?"

"So Gram said."

"I can imagine. What about Jennifer?"

"Gram said Jennifer was crying."

"I didn't mean to hurt anyone," she apologized.

"I know, but you did." I told her the truth. "How come you didn't wake me up after you talked to your mom? We could have talked. I understand what you're going through."

"No offense, Garrett, but I could tell by what you said last night that you don't."

"I wasn't thinking then, Leighla. Now I know what you're going through is something like what I went through with hockey in the sixth grade."

"Ice Hockey? You used to play hockey?"

"Hey, my father gave me a hockey stick for my second birthday. Dad had me skating backwards by the time I was three. I was on a hockey team when I was five. It was the most important thing in my life. Like I think modeling used to be for you. You used to like modeling once upon a time, right?"

"Of course. When I did it once in a while. Before the famous thing happened."

"When my father was young, he almost made it to the 'pro's,' " I explained. "He got to the major junior level. He was even drafted and went to a Philadelphia Flyers rookie tryout camp. But he didn't have the stuff to make the National Hockey League."

She looked confused.

"I'm telling you this because it was my father's ambition that Hornbeck or I would get the same chance and maybe one day would make the big league. So Dad had me on skates as soon as I could walk."

"Mom had me modeling when I was a baby," Leighla said. "I was in the Sears catalogue when I was a toddler."

"Your mom and my dad sound alike."

"Mom always wanted the famous thing more than me."

"Same here. I mean, I loved hockey and I was good at it. When I was eleven, I was playing on the top Peewee team in Vancouver. We'd go to tournaments all over the States and Canada. There are guys I played with who will be NHL stars someday."

Something splashed off the starboard bow.

"What was that?" Leighla asked.

"Some kind of fish," I answered. "Marlin maybe. Maybe a shark. Or maybe it was a dolphin. They come this far north."

"As long as it's not a . . . you know, as long as it's not one of those ghost ships." Leighla formed a feeble smile to show me she was making a feeble joke.

I smiled feebly back. "Anyway, about me and hockey. When I was playing with the elite team, the sport stopped being fun. It seemed all I did was play hockey. On the days we didn't have games, we'd practice. Every single day I had to go to the rink. And there was always pressure to win. The coach would bawl at us if we lost. Dad would holler at me if I made a mistake. It got to the point where I didn't want to go to the arena anymore. I wanted to quit."

"I don't ever want to go inside another TV studio," Leighla affirmed.

"So I told dad how I felt. I told him how miserable I was," I went on. "Dad just laughed it off. I told my coach; he said I was being a wimp. They didn't listen to me. You told your mom and you got the same reaction. She didn't listen."

"She doesn't understand."

"You're right, she doesn't. But it wasn't until I spoke to the school counselor I understood why. The counselor told me no matter how pushy my father was, how angry he got at me when I messed up, Dad thought he was doing what was best for me. He always wanted what *he* thought was the best for me."

"I wish I had a dollar for every time my mother has said that to me," Leighla confessed.

"And the coach didn't want me off his team, because I was one of his best players. That's just like Karl and Jennifer and your agency."

There was a moment of silence. "So you're saying I should speak to a counselor?"

"Somebody like that. Somebody who's neutral. The school counselor told me when it came to the bottom line, I was the one who had to make the decision. If I didn't want to play, then it wasn't right for other people to force me into it. The counselor called Dad and we had a big meeting. Dad didn't like it at first, and even though he was disappointed, we worked it out. I quit the triple-A team and joined the local rep team. I still got to play hockey but it was only once or twice a week. I started to like it again. There was no pressure. Maybe, if you talk to somebody, they can help you enjoy modeling again, Leighla. Maybe you could go to New York one week a month or something like that."

"You think it will help?"

"The counselor helped me."

"Maybe I could stop doing the TV work. I hate that. There's so much pressure."

"The way I took at it, *you're* the important person, Leighla. Without you, Karl and Jennifer don't have a job. Your agency doesn't make any money. You tell them what *you* want."

"Do you still play hockey?"

"This year I'm going to try out for the midget team in Bay of Bays. They're in the state league."

Her left hand squeezed my right hand. "Thank you, Garrett. I'm going to think about what you said. Maybe I'll do that. You've made me feel better." She paused. "And thank you for talking like you think we're going to get home safely."

I stared into the soupy haze. Don't think about what can happen, I thought to myself.

"Did you see our picture in the newspaper this morning?" I asked.

"No, but I'm not surprised it got into the paper so fast. Dennis doesn't waste any time."

"He kept his word," I told her about Fitzgerald's promise not to tell where she is. "All it says is you're someplace in Maine."

106

"Yeah, well, he's the last person I'm going to feel grateful to," she said sourly.

"It looks like we're kissing."

"Pardon."

"In the photo. You're leaning and checking the bug in my eye. It looks like we're about to kiss."

She let go of my hand and rubbed her forehead. "I can just hear what the people in my agency are saying right now. You must feel awfully embarrassed, Garrett."

"Butcher thinks I'm a cool dude now."

She chuckled.

"I don't know if Stacey will ever talk to me again, though."

"Who's Stacey?"

"My girlfriend. We've kind of been going out for a couple of weeks."

"Stacey was mad when she saw the picture in the paper?"

"Stacey came to Bed and Roses this morning. She wasn't angry. I guess you could say she was hurt."

"I'll talk to Stacey when we get back to Pirate Cove," Leighla promised. "I'll explain to her."

"Thanks," I said.

*If* we get back to Pirate Cove, I thought.

# chapter 9

We sat in silence once more, clinched in the embrace of my jean jacket. I thought how odd this was; how much like my imaginary igloo. Then I thought about what would happen in the near future. How we'd drift into the ocean currents. How it would get colder as it got darker, as we floated north. How, if the cold didn't get us by morning, we'd be thirsty. And if we spent another day lost in the fog or undiscovered, we'd be so thirsty we'd be desperate. And the thoughts certainly frightened me.

"Tell me about Pirate Cove," Leighla said.

"There isn't much to tell. You saw most of it out the window of our inn."

"It's such a pretty town. What's your school like?"

Making small talk sounded like a better idea

than brooding over what might happen. "Pirate Cove School is small. It goes from kindergarten to ninth grade, but there's only one class for each grade."

"Do you like your teacher?"

"Different teachers teach different subjects in junior high. But they're all okay. Especially Miss Scott. She's always telling us neat trivia stuff that nobody knows about."

"Like what?"

"Let's see. Like Madonna used to be a cheerleader in high school. Stuff like that."

"Madonna? No way."

"That's what Miss Scott said. She also told us someone paid over seven thousand dollars for Elvis Presley's first driving license. Dumb, huh?"

"Yeah," Leighla agreed. "Think of all the useful stuff you could buy with that much money."

"Speaking of silly people having too much money. You know those slippers Dorothy wore in *The Wizard of Oz,* the red ones she clicks to return to Kansas at the end of the movie? Miss Scott said they had an auction and someone paid a hundred sixty-five thousand buckaroonies for those. Mr. Manning, my English teacher, sent a letter to *Jeopardy* telling them they should have Miss Scott on the show. She's going to fly out to do a test audition."

"I can't watch *Jeopardy,*" Leighla said. "Especially when they have teen week. Every time I see the show, it makes me feel stupid. What's Mr. Manning like?"

"Mr. Manning is an old hippie. He has long hair like they did way back then. He walks around singing old rock songs and calling everyone "man." And I think he really likes Miss Scott. There's a rumor going around that they're dating."

"Your school sounds wonderful. Do you know I haven't been in a school since I was in the fifth grade? That's when I got my first big TV job, modeling for Kids Klothes. I still remember my first commercial and all that ice cream."

I thought for a moment. "That was you? You were that little skinny girl in the commercial who dropped the scoop of ice cream on her T-shirt?"

"That was me. At the time we were filming, I thought I was so lucky. We'd rehearse and they'd give me a fresh scoop of strawberry ice cream. By the time we finished the ad, I'd eaten half the bucket. A half minute after the last take, I threw up all over the same T-shirt."

"Wow, *you* were that little kid. You sure have changed."

"Sometimes I wish I was in the fifth grade again. Going to school. Doing normal, average, everyday things. Believe it or not, I really miss school."

"I believe it," I told her. "In June, I'm busting for summer break to begin. But by the end of August I can hardly wait for school to start again so I can see my friends after they've come home from vacation."

"Tell me about your friends," Leighla requested. "I remember having all kinds of friends back in fifth grade. What's it like in the eighth grade?"

"The same, I guess. You have good friends and you have once-in-a-while friends. My best friend is Delton. He's the only person I talk about personal stuff with. Del is superstitious, very superstitious. He keeps a little plastic rabbit in his pocket. He thinks if a rabbit's foot is good luck, then a whole rabbit must be better luck."

"Makes sense," she said.

I laughed to myself. "Last week Del got his foot caught in the toilet."

"He what?"

"One of our option classes is called 'Work Experience,'" I explained. "That's a fancy title for helping out. I help the third grade teacher put up art and mix paint and other gofer jobs. Delton helps Mr. O'Keeffe, the janitor. Last week Del was changing the light bulbs in the boys' bathroom. He stood up on a toilet to reach the fixture thing and slipped. His foot went straight into the toilet and he couldn't pull it out. They had to call nine-one-one. Del got carried out of school with a toilet on his foot. It was majorly funny."

Despite the cold, the fog, the increasing darkness, I couldn't help but laugh at the memory. And Leighla laughed along with me. Maybe we were laughing because we didn't want to think about how much trouble we were in.

"And there's Butcher," I continued. "In a way, he's a good buddy, too."

"He thinks you're a cool dude," she said.

"He thinks I'm a nerd, too."

"A nerd? That's the last thing you are."

"Thanks. My grandmother calls Butcher a character because he does weird stuff."

"Like what?"

"Where do I start? In the seventh grade, he was shooting spitballs with one of those straws that bend in the middle and he ended up shooting a spitball into his own ear. He had to go to the clinic to have it removed."

That made Leighla laugh even harder.

"At Outdoor Ed camp, Butcher brought a tube of skin cream instead of toothpaste by mistake. He brushed his teeth with skin cream for three days and spent the time complaining how greasy his mouth felt."

"Gross."

"Believe me, there's grosser stuff."

"I think I'd like to meet Butcher. He sounds very different."

"Yeah, Butcher is definitely different."

"You're so lucky. I'd really like friends like those," Leighla said. "Tell me about Stacey."

"In a way, she sort of looks a lot like you. Neat hair. Great green eyes. A super smile. She's into horoscopes and biorhythms and that stuff."

"It sounds like you really like her."

"Yeah, I do. Her dad is the horror writer, Dennis Queen. That's the name he writes under. His real name is Richard Bowman. He moved to Pirate Cove because it's a quiet place to write. And because Butcher's dad is a relative."

"Dennis Queen! That's awesome. I love his books."

"He said he was going to use my name for one of his characters in his next book."

"What a thrill. You'll be famous, Garrett."

"Like you."

"Yeah, like me." Leighla sounded sad. She paused and listened to the foghorns. They were now so soft, they'd almost faded away.

"Then there's Francine. She does these terrific imitations of things. She can sound like a jet engine. Or a popcorn popper. Or the dinosaurs from *Jurassic Park*. Or a toilet flushing in an airplane bathroom."

"This is sort of embarrassing, Garrett," Leighla

113

said meekly. "But speaking of bathrooms, I have to go to the bathroom. What do you do when you have to go to the bathroom out on the ocean like this?"

"The only thing you can do is go over the side of the boat."

"Oh," she said. "In that case, I'm pretty sure I can hold it. It would be more than embarrassing if another boat were close and they saw us."

What a silly thing to say, I thought. Another boat? In this fog? Even if there was another boat there's no way . . . "An aircraft carrier," I said out loud.

"An aircraft carrier?" Leighla puzzled.

"A little while ago, I was thinking that an aircraft carrier could be a few yards away and we wouldn't be able to see it because the fog is too thick. Well, it could, couldn't it?"

"What could?"

"There could be an aircraft carrier nearby. No, what I mean is, there could be a boat, a fishing boat, within shouting distance. It's a long shot, but who knows. A boat could be out there. Hello!" I yelled into the fog. "Help!"

"Wouldn't we hear the motor if there was a boat near us?" Leighla asked.

"Maybe not. First, this fog can kill the sound of an engine. Second, if the boat is drift fishing, the motor won't be on. Hey!" I yelled. "Is anybody out there?"

I listened for any response.

114

Nothing.

I noticed we couldn't hear the foghorns anymore. We were close to the deep sea currents now. Soon we'd start drifting north. At least the water isn't rough, I thought. Thank goodness for that.

"Hey, out there!" I hollered.

I realized there was a hundred-to-one chance there'd be a fishing boat near us. Heck, maybe the odds were a thousand to one. Ten thousand to one. Maybe more. But I also realized the only hope we had of being rescued, of getting out of this alive was getting someone to find us. Calling out was our only hope.

"We're here!" I hollered into the fog.

No response.

"We need help!" Leighla called.

And for a long time we shrieked and howled into the dreary, heavy murkiness. I'd yell and fifteen seconds later, Leighla would shout and we quickly fell into the rhythm, taking turns calling out SOS.

There was no response.

After awhile, Leighla stopped calling. "Why did you stop?" I asked.

"You'll think I'm silly," she answered. "It's just that the fog is so spooky and . . . you'll think I'm silly."

"What?"

"I started to think that maybe one of those

115

ghost ships will hear us," she said sheepishly. "I thought maybe those dead sailors would come and snatch us away. See, I told you it was silly."

"There's no way that story is real," I said. "But I understand why you feel that way. It *is* scary out here. And I just thought of something, anyway. Shouting like that was a useless thing to do. We'd be able to hear a nearby ship in this fog. The fishing boats all have foghorns. Most of them are on a timer, so they sound every minute or less. The chance of a couple of ships bonking each other isn't great. But it's still a chance."

"What do those horns sound like?"

"Like the one on Hole's Island."

"Really? There was one time you were shouting for help and I thought I heard the Hole's Island horn under your voice. Not very loud. I thought it was my imagination."

"When did you hear it?"

"Three or four minutes ago."

"You're probably right. And even on the slim chance it was a boat horn, because it wasn't loud, they wouldn't have been able to hear us. Stand next to a foghorn, it'll blow you off your feet."

She sighed. "I really do have to go to the . . . " She stopped in mid-sentence. "What's that? Garrett, there's something floating in the water. It's one of those things from the dock."

"A thing from the dock?" I struggled out of the

jacket, jumped up and peered into the ocean off Leighla's side, the port side. And through the mist, on the surface of the dark water, I saw an orange buoy with a large blue dot bobbing less than two feet away.

"Holy moley!" I exclaimed. "It's a lobster trap! I don't believe it!"

Incredible! It was one of Delton's dad's lobster traps. Instantly, I threw myself onto the gunwale, plunged my hand into the cold salt water and grabbed beneath the trap. My fingers encircled the quarter inch wire and I pulled. The plastic buoy only weighed a couple of pounds and I had no trouble yanking it out of the sea. I slipped as I stood up, fell, sprawled backward and knocked Leighla off-balance. She tumbled across the front seat. As I slipped, I bounced off her and slid onto the floor of *The Estelle*.

"Ooh," I moaned as I struggled.

"Oof!" she complained.

Leighla stayed flat out on the seat. I held the buoy like a basketball and I started laughing. "We're okay," I said between chuckles. "We're going to be fine. It's a lobster trap. It'll be our anchor."

As *The Estelle* continued to drift, the wire connecting the buoy to the trap on the ocean bottom suddenly tightened, almost snapping our good fortune out of my hands. I scrambled to tie the wire around one of the cleats.

117

"We won't float any further out to sea," I told her. "We'll wait for the tide to change, then we'll drift back in."

Leighla struggled to a sitting position and I hopped into the front seat and hugged her. This time I wasn't hugging to stay warm. This time it was a hug of congratulations.

"Garrett," Leighla said. "While I was flat out on the seat just then, I got an idea. The seat is made of wood."

I looked at the two teak boards which made up the seat. "Yeah, so?"

"If we knocked those loose, couldn't we use them as paddles? Maybe we can use the anchor to bang them off."

I planted a kiss on her cheek. "Leighla, you're a genius. As soon as the tide changes in another hour, we'll do that. It's tough to paddle a Joycraft, but it'll make the trip home shorter. Also it'll keep us warm. I'll . . ." I stopped speaking. "Do you hear something?"

Leighla tilted her head, like a dog does when it's listening. "I don't hear anything."

"Shush," I said. I turned my head left, then right, searching for the source of the sound. "Listen," I said. "Off your side. You hear that?"

She listened again. "No."

I pointed into the fog. "Right about there." I pointed. "Hear it? It's a motor."

"I can't hear any . . . wait," she said. "There. A soft thud-thud-thud."

"I think it's a diesel. A fishing boat motor. There's a boat out there, Leighla." I cupped my hands around my mouth. "We're over here!" I bellowed. "We're over here!"

The air was filled with a dull but loud horn.

"It's a ship's horn," I told Leighla. "There's a fishing ship out there."

"What if it's a ghost ship?" Leighla asked.

"Ghost ships don't have engines," I reasoned. "They don't have horns. There's a boat nearby. Help me call."

And to my surprise, Leighla began singing "Amazing Grace" in her loudest voice. *"Amazing grace, how sweet the sound . . ."*

"What are you doing?"

"I'm not taking any chances," she said. "If it's a ghost ship I want to make those dead sailors remember their families and forget about us."

So I joined her, bellowing at the top of my lungs. *". . . that saved a wretch like me."*

A light appeared in the fog.

*"I once was lost, but now I'm found."*

The sound of the motor got louder. The light grew brighter.

*"Was blind but now I see!"*

The motor cut and the light lit up the fog. The bow of a fishing boat floated beside us. I read her

119

name, *The Delton*. It was Del's father boat. "Mr. Hayes," I called. "Here!"

I could see the fuzzy image of Mr. Hayes directing the big deck light in our direction. "Garrett?" he shouted. "I'm so glad I found you. The Coast Guard sent out a mayday asking all craft to look for *The Estelle*."

"Am I ever glad to see you, Mr. Hayes." I tossed the tie rope to him and he pulled *The Estelle* alongside his fishing boat.

"Come aboard," he ordered. He held Leighla's hand as she boosted herself aboard *The Delton*. Then he supported me as I climbed aboard. Mr. Hayes's face was lined with puzzled frowns. "What are you youngsters doing out this deep in this fog?" he asked. "Why were you singing like that? I couldn't believe my ears."

"It started when . . ." I began.

"I'm sorry to interrupt," Leighla interrupted. "But is there a bathroom on board, sir?"

Mr. Hayes nodded. "The head is in the lower cabin."

"The head?"

"That's the bathroom on a boat," I explained.

"That's the door to the lower cabin," Mr. Hayes instructed.

Leighla smiled at us. "I'll be right back."

chapter 10

While Leighla used the head, I detailed the events of our adventure to Mr. Hayes. How we ran out of gas, drifted out with the tide, shared my jacket to stay warm, called out for other ships.

"That must be what I heard the first time," Mr. Hayes told me. "I was heading back to the harbor, and I thought I heard somebody shouting. So I circled back to make sure it wasn't my imagination. I don't think I would have turned back if I hadn't heard the Coast Guard's message."

"At one point, Leighla told me she thought she heard a horn."

"The odds of me being so close to you in this pea-souper is like finding a needle in a haystack. I'm certainly glad I came back," Mr. Hayes said.

Leighla emerged from the lower cabin. "I'm

glad you came back too, sir. I had to go to the bathroom real bad."

"Thanks, Mr. Hayes," I said. "It would have been hours before we'd have drifted back to shore. And who knows where we could have drifted. We could have landed halfway between Pirate Cove and Bay of Bays. Then we'd have been stuck out overnight with no fire."

Leighla frowned. "You didn't say anything about that, Garrett."

"That's because I thought we'd be off Nova Scotia by nightfall," I explained. "I didn't think we'd be lucky enough to find the lobster buoy."

"Let's untie that," Mr. Hayes said. "I'll get my trap and we'll tow *The Estelle* home." He squinted his eyes and leaned a little closer to Leighla. "I hope this doesn't sound rude, miss, but I'm sure I could almost swear my son, Delton, has a large poster of you on his wall."

"Delton has good taste when it comes to celebrities," I said. "Meet Leighla Livingston, Mr. Hayes."

Delton's father's mouth opened so wide that a bird could make a nest in it.

The first thing Mr. Hayes did was to use his marine radio to tell the authorities we were okay. After that we took care of the lobster buoy and *The Estelle,* then Leighla and I sat behind Mr.

122

Hayes in the heated upper cabin as he steered *The Delton* back to Pirate Cove. The three of us made small talk. I told Leighla more about my friends and Pirate Cove School and my folks and Hornbeck and some of my finest hockey moments. She told us about her family, some of the crazy things she and Tanya had done back in St. Albert before she became famous. She talked more about the modeling industry, how rotten it was, and gave a surprised Mr. Hayes a dozen more reasons why 'rich and famous' could be the pits. Delton's dad told us funny fishing stories and how lobster blood is blue. I wonder if Miss Scott knows that?

What we didn't talk about was what was waiting for us back in Pirate Cove. Gram and Karl and Jennifer and their reaction to everything.

And then we were home. Thanks to the foghorn and the dock lights, Mr. Hayes steered the boat to its berth on Big Dock. Then it was time to face the consequences. Gram, Jennifer and Karl, along with Sheriff Carson, were waiting on the boardwalk, looking suitably worried. And suitably angry. The sheriff told us we'd have to talk to the Coast Guard tomorrow. "You'll have to go through a complete debrief," is what the sheriff said.

We said another *thank you* to Mr. Hayes and walked the short distance to our house. To my surprise, none of the adults said anything until we opened the door to Bed & Roses. "Thank God," Gram exclaimed. "Thank God you're both safe."

Then we moved into the living room and an angry Karl explained how Mr. Glover had heard Leighla was missing and had told sheriff Carson what he knew. The police had gone to Hole's Island looking for us and when they couldn't find *The Estelle,* they guessed what had happened and knew we were in trouble. They contacted the Coast Guard who radioed all the local fishing boats to ask them to be on the lookout for us.

For a second time, I gave a play-by-play of our adventure. My words were punctuated by "Oh, my's" and "How lucky's" from the adults.

Gram hugged Leighla and me when I finished. "It was a miracle," she said.

Then Jennifer hugged us. "To think what could have happened if you hadn't found the lobster trap."

Karl's reaction was completely different. He gave us a three-minute lecture about how stupid we were. "I am extremely angry," Karl snapped. "This will not happen again."

"You're right," Leighla calmly said to him. "It won't. I'm sorry it happened this time. I was a little . . . a little confused, but Garrett and hockey have helped me sort a few things out." She smiled at her bodyguard. "Karl, if you want to stay with me, I want you to stop being so . . . so you. I appreciate your concern and the good job you do, but there's no way you're ever going to shout at me again."

"I . . ." The tough guy didn't know what to say. "This is . . ."

"Never again. I hope you understand."

"You . . ."

"Thanks, Karl," Leighla said. "Now I want you to get in touch with the father of Garrett's girlfriend and invite him and his daughter over. I'd like to meet him and tell him how much I enjoy his books. Also there's something I have to tell Stacey." She glanced at the grandfather clock. "School should be out in an hour. That should give you enough time to arrange it." She turned to Jennifer. "Jennifer, I want you to cancel all my shoots for the rest of the week. No, make that the rest of the month."

"Pardon?" Jennifer was shocked. "I can't do that."

"I'm sure you can. You just tell the agency I won't be there."

"But . . ."

"Garrett, where's the nearest big airport?" she asked me.

"Portland," I answered. "Or Fredericton in Canada."

She returned her attention to Jennifer. "Call

those two airports and find out the fastest way for me to fly back home."

"But the agency," Jennifer said.

"Tell the agency if they ever want me to model again, they're going to have to listen to what *I* want." She grinned in my direction.

"Go for it," I coached.

"Then I want you to phone my mother and tell her I'm coming home for a while and I want an appointment with Dr. Cheaney. She's the counselor my older sister went to. Would you do that, please, Jennifer?"

"A counselor?" Jennifer puzzled.

"I have a few things to work out. I'm going upstairs to take a bath now. Any questions?"

Jennifer and Karl regarded each other with dazed expressions.

Way to go, Leighla, I thought.

Jennifer noticed the newspaper on the coffee table, folded so our photograph in *The Estelle* was facing up. She picked it up, scanned it, then nodded. "You take a good picture, Garrett," she said. "If you want a job selling jeans, let me know. I'll speak to the people in the agency."

With Leighla in the tub, Jennifer went off to do her chores. I told Karl how to reach Mr. Bowman and he set out to complete the task. Gram and I went into the kitchen.

"Maybe you and Leighla should go see Doctor Jenkins," Gram said. "Have her check you out."

"I feel fine. And Leighla's good, too."

"You were out on the sea a long time. You must have been very frightened. It's cold. People can suffer from shock, you know."

"I'm okay," I said. "I just need a drink."

"A drink?"

"Milk. Warm milk. I need a mug of hot milk."

"Coming right up," she said.

I took a cookie from the cookie jar. "Gram, this is going to sound like a silly question, but are there any ghost stories about Bed & Roses?"

"I've been living in this house over fifty years," she answered as she zapped a cup of milk in the microwave. "And I've never heard or seen anything remotely ghostly. But there are a couple of curious stories."

"Like what?"

"Well, when I first turned the house into a bed and breakfast after your Grandpa died eighteen years ago, one of my first guests was a woman from Boston. She walked through the door and said, 'I'm psychic and I feel a presence here.' Just like that."

"That doesn't sound like much of a ghost story," I said through a mouthful of chocolate cookie crumbs.

"The next morning, the woman came down to

127

breakfast and said, 'I saw a presence at the top of the stairs. It's a girl, about ten years old. She was dressed in a white dress and lace-up boots."

Suddenly, I couldn't swallow and had to spit the cookie into a napkin.

The microwave dinged and Gram brought the steaming mug to the table. "I would have thought the woman was a little potty, if it wasn't for the roofer," she went on. "That was ten years ago now. Bed and Roses needed some roof repairs so I hired a gentleman from Bay of Bays. Since the job was going to take a few days, he decided to stay in your room, Third Floor Back, rather than commute. One morning he came down. He was shaking and told me he couldn't stay in the room anymore. He said he'd waked up and there'd been a young girl with straight black hair at the foot of his bed. The girl was pointing to her mouth as if she wanted to say something."

I coughed.

"That's curious, isn't it?" Gram observed. "I mean, both of them saw a young girl? Are you all right, Garrett? Garrett? Perhaps you should go see the doctor after all. You've gone all white."

Gram was amazed when I told her my story about the ghost girl.

"You believe I saw her?" I asked.

"I believe *you* believe you saw her. That's all that's important."

"That makes it sound like I'm nuts."

She laughed. "I never thought of that possibility."

"I find it hard to believe it was my imagination, Gram."

"Are you saying you find it easier to believe that what you saw was a ghost, Garrett?"

"I get your point, Gram."

After school, while Stacey was talking with Leighla and Mr. Bowman, I sat around the kitchen table with Hornbeck and Travis to have that "little talk."

"So come on, Garrett," Travis said impatiently. "Tell us about it. I want to know if all the stuff I heard is true."

"Okay," I started to tell them what I'd learned in sixth grade Health class. "Sometime in the next few years, you're going to go through a few changes." Fifteen minutes later I finished with, ". . . and that's all I know."

"Cool!" Travis said. "Cool! Isn't that neat, Hornbeck?"

Hornbeck had a disgusted look, like he'd just stepped in something. "You didn't just make that up, Garrett?"

"That's what my gym teacher, Mr. McDuff, told me."

"Eww. It's sort of yucky."

"That's a strange comment from someone who kisses a girl with a runny nose," I pointed out.

As Hornbeck and Travis were walking out the back door, Butcher Bortowski walked in. "Hey, Hawgood," he said.

"Hi. How's your hearing now?"

"Good. The buzzing has stopped. Is Leighla Livingston here?"

I nodded. "She's in the sitting room, talking to Stacey."

He helped himself to a soda from the fridge and sat at the table. "Talking? After that picture in the paper? I wouldn't think they'd have much to talk about. Can I meet Leighla?"

"Sure. In fact, she wants to meet you."

"She does? Cool."

"Promise me you won't say or do anything stupid?"

"Me? Say something stupid? 'Course not. How come you weren't in school today? You sick?"

I told him about our adventure on the ocean.

"Go back a bit," Butcher said, after I finished the tale. "Did I hear right? You and Leighla Livingston shared a jacket? You hugged?"

"For over an hour."

"Wow. How come a nerd like you is so lucky?"

"Butcher, sometimes you're such a jerk," I teased.

He chuckled, then belched. "I got to be me."

Stacey and Leighla entered the kitchen. To my surprise, they both wore happy faces. Extremely happy faces. Butcher jumped to his feet. "It's you," he said to Leighla. "Too much! I dream you and me are stuck on a deserted island and we got nothing to wear but leaves and . . ."

"Butcher," I reminded him. "Remember your promise."

He shot me a quick look, then refocused on Leighla. "I'm pleased to meet you," he said politely. "I like your commercials. My name is Butcher."

"Ah, the boy who shoots spitballs into his own ears?" Leighla asked.

"How do you know about that?"

"I feel like I know you already, Butcher."

"You do? Great. Would you like to come to my house and see my collection of eyeballs? I don't live too far away. Just a couple of blocks."

"Eyeballs?" Leighla replied squeamishly.

"Yeah, I collect eyeballs."

"How?" Leighla wondered.

"I don't get them myself. I send away to science supply companies. I'm into biology in a big way.

131

I want to be a doctor when I finish school. Some kind of surgeon. Maybe operate on brains."

"That's interesting." Leighla sounded like she didn't believe her own words.

"So you want to come see my eyeballs?"

"Why not?" she said. "I'm not leaving until tomorrow. I think Garrett and Stacey would like to be alone. Let me tell Karl where I'm going."

"Karl?" Butcher asked. "Is that your bodyguard?"

"Let's just say he looks out for me. A little."

"Well, you tell him not to worry because you'll be with me. If someone tries to take your photo, I'll take the camera and eat the film."

"And he probably will," I added.

"We'll see you guys later," Leighla said to Stacey and me as she guided Butcher out of the kitchen.

"Butcher is in heaven," I said.

Stacey walked over and planted a kiss on my cheek. "Me too," she said. "Leighla explained everything to me. About the bug in your eye. How much you talked about me. And that you guys don't even like each other."

"She said that?"

"Not that you don't like each other. Just that you don't like each other like you and I like each other."

I think I understood that.

132

"I should have listened to you this morning. I should have known there was a reason. And I should have guessed Leighla is a Leo. Aries have a soft spot for Leos."

"It won't happen again, Stacey."

"It probably will," she disagreed. "You're an Aries. You tend to jump into things without thinking."

"Did everyone at school give you a hard time about the picture in the paper?"

"No. I thought I'd get teased about it, but exactly the opposite happened," she said. "Most of the girls came up to me and said, 'Garrett must be something special if Leighla kissed him.' I had to keep telling them I already knew you were special."

Her father entered the kitchen, laughing to himself. "I don't think I've seen anything so funny in a long time," Mr. Bowman chuckled.

"What? What are you laughing at, Dad?" Stacey asked.

"Your video," Mr. B answered. "Hornbeck showed it to me. I watched Butcher and Baker do their 'Bill and Ben, the Trash Can Men' thing."

"That's funny," I said.

"Funnier still is when Travis and his friends belly'd the camera," Mr. Bowman observed with a smile.

"Guys," Stacey said. "I'll never understand."

\*     \*     \*

That night, in bed, I thought about the day, about how lucky Leighla and I had been in *The Estelle*. Leighla returned from Butcher's quite impressed by the big guy's eyeball collection. She told me that she and Butcher were going to become pen pals. *Very interesting*. Stacey and Leighla spent the evening filming each other on the video for my folks. By the end of the night, they were acting like close friends. They, too, promised to keep in touch. Leighla invited Stacey to spend some time with her in New York once she "sorted things out." As I was falling asleep, I pictured myself in an igloo in the middle of an arctic blizzard.

*I'm sharing the ice block house with Stacey and Leighla.*

*"Oh, Garrett," Stacey and Leighla say in my imagination. "We're so frightened."*

*"There's no problem," I assure them. "The blizzard will be over in a week or two."*

*"Whatever are we going to do for all that time?" Stacey and Leighla wonder.*

*"We'll think of something," I answer.*

*"It's so cold in here." They shiver.*

*"Say, I have a jacket," I suggest.*

*"I'm not cold," Stacey says.*

*"Me neither," Leighla agrees.*

\* \* \*

Poof. My fantasy vanished.

Oh well, I thought. Someday my fantasy will work out okay.

I looked around the gloom of my room, thinking that maybe I'd see the girl I'd seen twice that day, a girl seen by two of our guests.

Nothing.

I fell asleep with the feeling I'd meet her again.

# Look for All the Unforgettable Stories by Newbery Honor Author

★ **AVI** ★

THE TRUE CONFESSIONS OF CHARLOTTE DOYLE
71475-2/ $4.50 US/ $5.99 Can

NOTHING BUT THE TRUTH       71907-X/ $4.50 US/ $5.99 Can

THE MAN WHO WAS POE         71192-3/ $4.50 US/ $5.99 Can

SOMETHING UPSTAIRS          70853-1/ $4.50 US/ $6.50 Can

PUNCH WITH JUDY             72253-4/ $3.99 US/ $4.99 Can

A PLACE CALLED UGLY         72423-5/ $4.50 US/ $5.99 Can

SOMETIMES I THINK I HEAR MY NAME
72424-3/$3.99 US/ $4.99 Can

───────── *And Don't Miss* ─────────

ROMEO AND JULIET TOGETHER (AND ALIVE!) AT LAST
70525-7/ $3.99 US/ $4.99 Can

S.O.R. LOSERS              69993-1/ $4.50 US / $5.99 Can

WINDCATCHER                71805-7/ $4.50 US/ $6.50 Can

BLUE HERON                 72043-4 / $3.99 US/ $4.99 Can

"WHO WAS THAT MASKED MAN, ANYWAY?"
72113-9 / $3.99 US/ $4.99 Can

# IF YOU DARE TO BE SCARED...
# READ SPINETINGLERS!
## by M.T. COFFIN